THE BETTER
THE QUESTIONS,
THE BETTER THE GAME...

"Hey, guys, I have a great idea. Let's play Skeletons in the Closet."

"What's that?" Brenda asked cautiously. She had a bad feeling about this, but could see no way to stop the game from happening if the other girls were interested. She didn't want to look like a wuss.

Eagerly, Amanda explained, "Everyone sits in a circle, and the person in the middle has to answer all our questions as honestly as possible."

Brenda glanced at Kelly, who seemed apprehensive. "What kind of questions?" Brenda asked anxiously.

"Any kind," Amanda said. "Of course, the better the questions, the better the game."

BEVERLY 90210 HILLS ™

SPELLING ENT. INC.

NO SECRETS

A novel by
Mel Gilden

From teleplays by Darren Star, Karen Rosin,
and Jordan Budde

Based on the television series created by
Darren Star

HarperPaperbacks
A Division of HarperCollinsPublishers

HarperPaperbacks *A Division of* HarperCollins*Publishers*
10 East 53rd Street, New York, N.Y. 10022

Copyright © 1992 by Torand, a Spelling Entertainment Company
All rights reserved. No part of this book may be used or reproduced in any manner whatsoever without written permission of the publisher, except in the case of brief quotations embodied in critical articles and reviews. For information address HarperCollins*Publishers,*
10 East 53rd Street, New York, N.Y. 10022.

Cover photos by Andrew Semel
Bac cover photo by Timothy White
Insert photos by Andrew Semel and Timothy White

First printing: February 1992

Printed in the United States of America

HarperPaperbacks and colophon are trademarks of
HarperCollins*Publishers*

❖ 10 9 8 7 6 5 4

Contents

1

Popping up

IN THE TERRIBLE BEVERLY HILLS HEAT, shimmering devils danced in the street, and even the big stucco houses looked somehow unreal, like movie sets. The sky was a hard, flat blue holding the white-hot marble of the sun.

Brenda Walsh felt sweaty and gritty. Her clothes stuck to her body. Wisps of long dark hair stuck to her face. She was positive that weather during the school year should not be like this. It certainly never had been this way back in Minnesota, where her family came from. One of the few advantages of living in Minneapolis as opposed to Beverly Hills was that you would not melt while walking home from the video store during November.

She stopped before attempting to walk up the gentle incline of the driveway, and just stood there breathing in and out the hot soup of the atmosphere. Up near the garage her brother, Brandon, leaned far under the hood of his car. His feet kicked the air as if he were attempting to swim down into the depths of the engine. She didn't know how he could work in this weather.

Brandon called his car Mondale. It was a few years old, and worse yet, it was a boxy blue Japanese thing—hardly the car of choice even among high-school kids in Beverly Hills. Life was difficult when your parents were not rich.

Brenda struggled up the driveway and sank gratefully into the shade of a big old tree. Ineffectually, she fanned herself with one hand. More to herself than to Brandon, she said, "Where is winter, already? I need a season I can sulk and be depressed in."

Brandon wriggled out of the engine compartment and, while he tossed a screwdriver, said, "Don't tell me, Bren. You're baby-sitting tonight and all the video stores were out of *Dirty Dancing*."

"I had to go to three places before I found it." The thought frustrated her all over again, but raising her voice was too great an effort.

Brandon really looked disgusting. To start with, the T-shirt he was wearing was full of holes; it must have been the oldest one in his drawer. Then, grease had been liberally applied. Sweat stains spread under his arms and down his front. He was a fragrant mess. "You must have that movie memorized by now," he said.

"Whatever gets you through the night. Isn't that what you always say?"

The sound of metal rollers came from under the car, and Dylan McKay slid out on a mechanic's trolley. "No, that's what *I* always say," he said with a smirk.

This was terrible. Here she'd been mentally criticizing Brandon for his appearance, but after her walk to the video stores she looked almost as bad as he did. Without the grease, of course. But enough sweat was soaked into her West Beverly High T-shirt to float battleships. "Er, hi. I didn't see you."

"I saw you."

Great. Say something, dummy. But before she had a chance to open her mouth again, her mother called from the house that Brenda had a phone call. Saved by the bell.

"Excuse me," Brenda said. "Probably a very important call from the president."

As she walked into the house she lamented the fact that she was wearing her old baggy jeans instead of something a little more chic. Inside, the house was dim and cool. Her mother looked very comfortable in shorts and a cotton shirt. The sweat actually felt cold against Brenda's skin.

She dropped *Dirty Dancing* on the kitchen table and eagerly picked up the phone. At the other end was Mrs. Ross, Katie's mom. Mr. and Mrs. Ross would not need Brenda's baby-sitting services that evening. Katie had chicken pox, and the Ross family was staying home.

Brenda nodded philosophically. First Dylan saw her at her absolute worst, and now her baby-sitting job fell through. She had spent the entire afternoon hunting for *Dirty Dancing* for nothing.

If she were not to spend the evening at home playing Scrabble with her parents—a thought that made her shudder—she had to make other plans fast. There was only one thing to do. She went upstairs, and in the privacy of her room called Kelly Taylor.

Kelly was a lithe, beautiful blonde who had taken Brenda under her well-manicured wing when the Walshes had first arrived from Minnesota. As the weeks and months had gone by, Kelly had taught Brenda how the social game was played at Beverly Hills High. They were very good friends, maybe even best friends.

While the phone rang, Brenda girded herself for the unpleasant task to come. Kelly answered the phone and Brenda hesitated, then said, "All right. I'll do it. I'll go out with your dweeb cousin Algernon."

"That's okay," said Kelly. "I convinced Donna to do it."

Donna was the third member of their core set. She had some learning problems and was perhaps not as bright as Kelly or Brenda, but she was really very nice: a knockout blonde with a killer figure. Brenda was disappointed to hear that Donna had agreed to do the deed. Even going out with Algernon would have been better than nothing.

"Want to come over?" Kelly asked.

The air was hot. Brenda was disgusted. Maybe she would watch *Dirty Dancing* after all. "No," she said shortly. "I think I'll just stay home and organize my sock drawer."

"You don't sound good, Brenda. You need a bubble bath."

Sure. A bubble bath, a date with Tom Cruise, a major credit card with no limit, the list went on and on. She and Kelly talked for a while longer, but Brenda's heart wasn't in it. They hung up and Brenda sat on her bed tapping on *Dirty Dancing* and listening to somebody racing Mondale's engine.

The engine dropped into a purr and

Brandon said, "Hey, Dad. Check this out. This baby is humming."

Curious, Brenda went to the window and looked down. Her dad, Brandon, and Dylan were standing around admiring Mondale. Brandon and Dylan were wiping their hands on rags that were nearly as dirty as what they were trying to clean.

Mr. Walsh peered at Dylan and said, "So, where'd you learn to work on cars?"

Dylan shrugged. He was kind of cute when he did that. "From working on cars, I guess. Same as Brandon."

"Except that Dylan has a Porsche," Brandon said.

Mr. Walsh nodded as if he understood. "Nice car," he said.

Brenda recognized the tone of voice her father was using. He didn't like Dylan and he was looking for evidence to support his feelings. When he said "nice car," what he really meant was, "too nice a car for a kid your age."

Mr. Walsh continued, pushing his way further out of bounds. "Bought it with your paper-route earnings, did you?"

Dad could be such a jerk. Brenda didn't want to listen anymore. She would have closed the window, but the breeze was nice. She wondered if there was any grape soda in the refrigerator. Actually a grape soda and a bubble bath sounded pretty good. As she walked out of her room Dylan's soft laughter faded behind her.

But when Brenda came back from the kitchen, grape soda in hand, Brandon was already in the bathroom, and steam from the shower was pouring into her room through the half-open door. "Brandon!"

The shower stopped and Brenda yelled into the bathroom, "Can't you shut the door? It's hot enough in here already—oh!"

Looking at her around the shower curtain was not Brandon but Dylan. He smiled and said, "Sorry," as Brenda backed quickly from the room and leaned the door closed, a little breathless.

She was not just embarrassed. She was excited, too. Dylan was *so* gorgeous. And here he was in her actual shower. She would never have gone so far as to plan such a thing, but she saw nothing wrong with enjoying it now that it had happened. She called through the door, "You keep popping up on me today."

"Who popped up on who?"

Brenda hugged herself. This was great. He was flirting with her.

"You like any movies besides *Dirty Dancing*?" he called out.

"Some," she said cautiously.

"Ever see *Animal Crackers*?"

"Is that a movie or a snack?"

"It's a Marx Brothers comedy. And if you've never seen it on the big screen, you're really missing something. Too bad you're working tonight."

"Actually my clients chickened out. I'm free." She labored mightily not to sound too eager.

"Great. Want to come with me and Brandon?"

Did she? Did she ever? "I'm there," she said casually. She leaped into the air, pumped one arm and mouthed a silent *yes!*

Brenda would have liked to ride in Dylan's Porsche, but Brandon insisted on giving Mondale a test drive. The guys' discussion about auto mechanics made a pleasant babble in the background while the cool evening air blew into Brenda's face through the open window.

She wondered what Dylan was really like and whether he could ever be interested in a girl like her. She knew he had a reputation for being wild and dangerous, but Brandon seemed to like him and that was usually a good sign. Actually, she could use a little wildness in her life about now. She had frightened herself badly when she had actually offered to go out with Kelly's cousin Algernon.

They arrived at the mall where the theater

was and Brenda enjoyed the dry comments Dylan made about the people who walked by while they waited in line. But her fun was cut short by the approach of a young woman heading straight toward Dylan.

She was surprised by how jealous she felt. After all, she and Dylan had barely met. She certainly had no claim on him. And yet, when he spoke with the absolutely awesome blonde who seemed to know him (Brandon was frankly fascinated), Brenda took Dylan's arm and held it till the other girl left.

Brandon continued to watch the sway of the awesome blonde as she threaded her way through the crowd. Without looking away, he casually asked, "Friend of yours?"

"Yeah, we used to hang out," Dylan said. "I'd introduce you, but I forgot her name."

"Terrific," Brenda said sarcastically.

"Not my fault," Dylan said. "She kept changing it. She was Tanya for a while. And then Rainbow. For a while she called herself Millicent. Who can blame the poor kid? I think her real name is something like Gertrude, or Beatrice, or Brenda."

Brenda was pretty sure Dylan was just kidding, but just to show she was paying attention, she punched him in the arm, hard.

Dylan gingerly rubbed the spot she'd hit and chuckled. "Mean right hook."

Brandon had been smiling for some time. He said, "Yeah. And who do you think she practices on?"

The Marx Brothers were as funny as Dylan had promised, though Brenda thought their attitude toward women needed a little adjustment. After the show Brandon drove while Dylan guided them to an exclusive complex of condos in the hills above Beverly Hills. It was a thing of beauty hidden among stone walls and dwarf palm trees.

They left Brandon's car with the man on duty and went up in the elevator to the McKay condo. Inside, it was furnished in ostentatious good taste. Glass walls looked out on what might have been primeval forest, but had probably been installed by a landscaping company. A fireplace big enough to house a family of four dominated the living room. Dylan chose a few compact discs from a library of hundreds and put one of them into the player. Music boomed from all around them. The sound quality was so good, the music did not seem to be recorded at all, but live. Dylan put the good sounds down to the quality of the sub-woofers, the hyper-tweeters, and the midrange boffers.

When Dylan went to answer the doorbell (it rang a little riff by Bach), Brenda took the

opportunity to say to Brandon, "Thanks for letting me come with you guys."

"If you play your cards right, we might do it
again." He winked at her. Dylan walked back
into the room carrying a big cardboard box
that brought with it the odors of hot grease and
grilled meat. "What do you say, McKay?"
Brandon asked.

Dylan opened the box and said,
"Absolutely," as he unloaded a mountain of
burgers, curly fries, and foil pillows of catsup.
Next to the mountain he stood silos—the large
economy-size cups—of cola. Fat and sugar,
Brenda thought. Death to summer figures and
clear complexions. This did not seem to be the
moment to worry about such things. She dug in
with the boys.

Brandon nibbled the fries and said, "These
are great. Just like the ones Henry makes at
your hotel."

"They *are* Henry's. He sends them over
since my dad closed the suite. He knows I can't
survive without my fix."

"What happened to the suite?"

Dylan shifted his position on the floor and
shrugged. "Long story," he said as if he was not
inclined to tell it.

"You stay here all by yourself?" Brenda
asked, and then regretted it. It sounded so
tacky.

But Dylan took up the challenge. He said, "Not always," and smiled lazily. He rose suddenly and swept a stack of CDs off the table. He held them out to Brenda like a magician asking a sucker to pick a card, and said, "Your turn to chose."

What Brenda wanted was not among the CDs in Dylan's hands. It wasn't a CD at all. But at the moment her choice was also her deepest secret.

2

Family reunion

AT SCHOOL ON MONDAY BRENDA HAD A tough time convincing Kelly that she had not been on a date with Dylan McKay. "I was just tagging along," Brenda said. "Really." Like everyone else, they were trying to get from one class to another without being trampled to death.

Maybe Brenda couldn't convince Kelly because she was having a tough time convincing herself. Actually, she enjoyed Kelly's misconception and wished it were true.

"Dylan McKay doesn't waste his time with just anybody," Kelly said emphatically. "He is known as a man of *action*, if you know what I mean."

Kelly reminded Brenda of Groucho Marx when she wiggled her eyebrows suggestively. "I would have to be living in a convent not to know what you mean," said Brenda. "But what you mean doesn't matter. I'm not even Dylan's type."

Kelly smiled confidently and said, "We can work on that."

At the moment Brenda was more concerned about getting through a class known as health. In health, Mr. Kravitz told them about the four basic food groups—which Steve Sanders insisted meant canned, frozen, instant, and spoiled—the importance of personal hygiene, and the evils of recreational drugs.

The big deal was Chapter Eleven, which dealt with sex. Mr. Kravitz reminded them constantly that they needed a signed parental consent form before they could learn about sex. For some of her friends, Brenda knew, it was a little late to be concerned about parental consent.

While Mr. Kravitz went on about parental-consent forms, Steve leaned across to Brenda and whispered, "Have you noticed that whenever Mr. Kravitz talks about sex, he starts stroking his beard?"

Brenda thought that Steve was just being a jerk, as usual, but she saw that he was right. Once you noticed what Mr. Kravitz was doing, you couldn't help being fascinated. The bell rang and Mr. Kravitz's voice was lost in the sound of stampeding bodies heading out the door.

After class Steve asked if she and Brandon wanted to come to a party he was throwing that weekend. Brenda doubted very much if parental-consent forms were required. As politely as she could manage, she told him that she and Brandon would be busy. Steve waited patiently to hear what they would be doing, but Brenda didn't tell him. With her books clutched in her arms, she turned down the nearly empty hallway and headed for her next class.

On Friday afternoon Brandon came home from school with red-rimmed eyes and a puffy face. Concerned, his mom got him into a bathrobe—the fuzzy one he liked to wear when he was not feeling well—and set him up with cup after cup of hot tea with lemon and honey.

He sneezed often, but this provided only a momentary relief. Piles of used tissue grew around him on the couch in the living room. Nothing actually hurt, but sneezing became a drag. He knew how. Why should he have to keep practicing?

The worst part was that he would not be able to go out that night with Brenda and Dylan. In other words Brenda and Dylan would be going out alone. In other words they would be alone together. Brandon liked him, but Dylan had that wild reputation. On the other hand, Dylan wouldn't do anything to jeopardize their friendship. Would he? Lighten up, Walsh, Brandon told himself. Dylan wasn't an animal. If worse came to worst, Brenda had that mean right hook, and Dylan knew it.

Brenda stood before him in a nice sweater and jeans—nothing too extreme, nothing too weird. Brandon sneezed, and Brenda and his mom blessed him.

"Hope you feel better," Brenda said.

"Someday, maybe. Why don't you and Dylan hang out here tonight? You can be the nurse and Dylan can be the orderly. It'll be fun." He sneezed. Mom and Brenda blessed him.

Brenda shook her head and said, "You don't want *us* to get sick, do you?"

Outside, a car pulled up and gave two jaunty honks. "There he is," Brenda said, more delighted than she had to be as far as Brandon was concerned. Brenda kissed her mom on the cheek, said, "Bye-yee" to her dad in the foyer, and was out the door in a flash. The Brenda Walsh flash.

Mr. Walsh came into the living room looking a little bewildered. He said, "Brenda isn't going out with that guy alone."

"Apparently." Mrs. Walsh did not sound concerned.

Mr. Walsh shook his head. "His father is known in financial circles as an unethical bastard. And that's in *polite* financial circles."

"Lighten up, Dad," Brandon said. He sniffled. "Dylan and his dad are two different people."

Unconvinced, Mr. Walsh said, "In my experience the apple doesn't fall very far from the tree."

Brandon was about to say something more in Dylan's defense, but the moment was lost when he had another sneezing fit.

Brenda and Dylan waited in the middle of a very long line. Their chances of getting into this hour's showing of the movie were two: slim and none. But waiting in line with Dylan was fun. He was a great student of people and he always had an interesting comment to make. Were those two in their second marriage? Was that a first date in progress? Brenda had no way of knowing if Dylan's analyses were correct, of course, but his explanations sounded plausible.

Brenda said, "You know a lot about this couples stuff."

"Don't you?"

Brenda was a little embarrassed by the question. She and Dylan were about the same age, but you couldn't always measure maturity in years. "I don't know," she said. "Not really, I guess."

Dylan looked at her for a long time without saying anything. His expression was unreadable. Did she have a wart on her nose, or what? At last he smiled. "What say we shine on this movie?"

Was Dylan making his big move? Would she be found pregnant in a flat in the slums of Cairo after a night of insane adventure? Or was he just some nice high-school guy she had attracted, and now she was getting the attention she'd hoped for? She felt herself smiling. "Sure," she said. "What do you have in mind?"

What Dylan had in mind was another session at his dad's condo. Only this time Brandon wouldn't be there as unofficial chaperon. Still, Brenda felt that to be fair, she had to give Dylan his best shot. There was a good chance that he wouldn't be a jerk. And if he was, well, cabs and telephones were everywhere.

But when they arrived at the condo, the situation changed radically in a way Brenda would never have guessed. Dylan opened the door, and immediately stopped, causing her to stop immediately behind him. Voices came from someplace deeper in the condo, and they did not make Dylan happy.

Dylan seemed to be in a trance as he walked down the hall to a door. Calculating male voices came from behind it. Dylan opened the door and Brenda caught a glimpse of four or five middle-aged men sitting around a big table in their shirt sleeves. Their ties were loose and their jackets were draped over the backs of chairs. Papers were scattered around the big table. A big man strode toward them and cried, "Dylan!" Apparently, Dylan was no more welcome than a cockroach.

Making the best of the situation, Dylan said, "Dad! When did you get back in town?"

Mr. McKay said, "I need to talk to you, boy," and pulled Dylan into the room. The man barely glanced at Brenda before he firmly shut the door.

Inside the room Dylan and his father spoke. Their voices rose into shouts and fell again. The argument seemed to be interminable, though according to Brenda's watch, only minutes had passed.

She didn't know what to do. It would be rude to leave. Besides, she felt that by staying she was showing Dylan a certain amount of support. Still, this was obviously personal family business. She wondered how she would feel if her own dad were ragging on her while Dylan waited downstairs. The shouting made her nervous.

She sat down. She stood up. There was a phone on a side table. Maybe she should call a cab and hope that she could explain her actions to Dylan some other time.

Then the fateful door opened and Dylan came out as if he'd been shot from a cannon. Obviously upset, he marched to a wet bar and poured himself a splash of brown liquid from a square-cut bottle. He noticed her, offered her a hit from the glass, and took another drink before she had a chance to decline.

"I didn't know you drank, Dylan."

"It's kind of a special thing we save for family reunions." He sounded angry. Would driving with him be safe, even if he didn't drink anymore?

She touched his drinking arm and said, "Come on, Dylan, don't. You have to drive me home."

He slammed down the drink and marched toward the front door. "Let's get out of here."

Brenda was confused by the abruptness of Dylan's actions. The elevator took forever to come, and in that time Brenda tried to sort out what had just happened. The people in her family sometimes got angry, but they never got *this* angry. She decided it could never hurt to be sympathetic. She said, "I don't know what happened in there—"

"That's right," Dylan said in a nasty way, "you don't."

"If you'd let me finish—"

"Excuse me. I seem to have a knack for interrupting things. And I've had about enough of that noise for one night! Is that okay with you?"

Brenda was surprised by Dylan's behavior. She'd had about enough of certain noise herself. She said nothing when the elevator arrived at last and they descended to the garage level. Dylan stood with his back to her while he waited for one of the valets to get his Porsche.

Brenda turned to the other valet and said, "Would you call me a taxi, please?"

Dylan whirled on her as if she'd attacked him. "You don't need a taxi. I'll be okay."

He didn't look okay to her. He looked crazy and dangerous.

"I want a taxi."

"No. Just come on now, dammit!" He grabbed her wrist, but she twisted away.

Frustration, anger, and confusion had brought Brenda to tears. "Don't you yell at me," she cried.

Dylan turned, looking for something to lash out at, and punched a hole in an enormous ceramic planter. Terrified by his outburst of violence, Brenda ran out of the garage and down the dark street toward the light at the bottom of the hill.

3

Connection

BRENDA HEARD RUNNING BEHIND HER and she knew Dylan was after her. The rumors about him had been right. She ran faster and discovered she was in terrible shape. Her breath came in great gasps. Thank goodness she'd decided to wear her running shoes instead of her heels.

The footsteps behind her got closer, and suddenly he had his arms around her. Terrified, she tried to fling him off. They struggled while Brenda shrieked at him to let her go.

"Brenda, please."

The tone of Dylan's voice made Brenda

stop. He sounded frightened and tired, as if she had surprised him by running away as much as he had surprised her with his violence. Still he did not let her go. He said, "I'm an idiot, Brenda. Please don't leave."

"You scare me."

"I'm sorry. I scare myself." He let go of her and leaned against a white stucco wall that gleamed like silver in the moonlight. He could not hurt her now. His strength was gone.

"Dylan, what happened?"

Without turning around, Dylan said, "He just gets to me. He always gets to me." He shook his head and hit the wall softly with his fist over and over again.

Brenda came around his other side so they could talk face-to-face. This was one strange confused guy. Could she help him? Did she want to try? Was he worth it?

"Please don't leave me," Dylan said.

He came into her arms like a frightened little boy. Into her shoulder he said, "I don't know what I'm supposed to do. I didn't want to . . ."

Brenda comforted him with cooing noises, as her mother had done for her during bad times. He kissed her, first as a brother might kiss a sister, then with more passion, and at last they abandoned themselves to it. This felt very good to Brenda. This felt right.

After a long time, Brenda suggested in a

small voice that Dylan take her home. Dylan chuckled. "I guess we should have stayed for the movie," he said.

As they walked back up the darkened hill to the condo garage, Brenda said, "No, I'm glad this happened."

Dylan shot her a surprised look.

Embarrassed, Brenda said, "No. I mean, I feel like I know some things about you not many other people know."

Dylan agreed.

"Tell me about it. About you and him."

Dylan didn't say anything for a long time and Brenda thought she'd made a mistake asking. But she didn't ask out of idle curiosity. She'd already seen a side of Dylan McKay this evening that told her he was more than just a spoiled rich kid who thought he was tough. That stuff made him more real and very desirable—desirable not only physically, but emotionally and intellectually. She wanted to see more. Was this love?

Then, Dylan began to talk. He told a long, twisted tale about a nasty divorce that had left him feeling the breakup of his parents had been his fault, about a mom who never called or wrote, about a dad who was more interested in his business than in his own son.

"The only way I got his attention was when

I did something wrong. It took me a long time to realize that I was only hurting myself. Then I began to criticize his business practices."

"What about his business practices?"

"I don't understand it all myself. Let's just say that what he did went way beyond keeping two sets of books."

Dylan pulled his Porsche up into the Walsh driveway and turned off the engine. The night was still. The house was dark.

Brenda listened as he continued the story of his life. With their fingers they made little circles on the backs of each other's hands. Brenda liked Dylan a lot. He had been through some bad times, not all of which were over. Few guys his age would have the intelligence or sensitivity to even begin to deal with this stuff. Dylan was something special, that was for sure. And if he didn't feel the same way about her, would he tell her all this personal stuff?

Dylan sighed. "After he kicked me out, we didn't talk for about a year. The situation has improved, but it's still no picnic."

Brenda shook her head. "I can't imagine being cut off like that. I talk to my parents about everything."

"Everything?" Dylan said, and smiled. He had such a nice smile.

"Well, *almost* everything."

They shared a small laugh. Then they

reached out for each other and once more
Brenda was lost in Dylan's embrace. He pulled
away for a moment and whispered, "Please
don't tell Brandon I lost my cool, okay?"

"Your secret, all your secrets, are safe with
me."

In school on Monday, Kelly tried to pump
Brenda for every detail of her date with Dylan.
Brenda was evasive. Still, Kelly felt obligated to
advise her. Brenda agreed to study at her
house that evening, though she doubted much
schoolwork would get done. She resolved not
to tell Kelly any of Dylan's personal history. It
was a sacred trust.

In health class, Mr. Kravitz reminded them
for about the millionth time that he needed
signed consent forms before they could partici-
pate in the sex part of the class. Brenda noticed
again that Steve Sanders was right: whenever
he talked about sex, Mr. Kravitz stroked his
beard. Was that Freudian or what? Then, he
showed the class five pounds of fat. Brenda
promised herself that she would never again
allow ice cream or french fries to pass her lips.

After class, she met Brandon in the hallway,
and while they walked to their lockers he kept
glancing at her as if she were some kind of natural curiosity, like a three-headed lizard or
something. She knew he wanted to ask her
about Dylan, and she wished he'd do it already

so she could deflect his questions and be done with it.

Dylan emerged from the crowd and Brenda felt warm inside. She could not help smiling. He said, "Yo, Brandon. How's the cold?"

"About gone, thanks. How was the movie? Brenda's a little vague on the subject."

Brandon was smiling at Dylan, but the expression looked plastered on. Here it was, Brenda thought. The moment of truth. She did her best to stay cool. At least Dylan was here to help.

"We, uh, didn't make the movie."

Brenda moved over to Dylan and put her arm around his waist, causing Brandon's eyes to widen. "It's no big deal, is it?" Brenda asked.

Brandon thought about that for a moment while he looked from Brenda to Dylan. "I guess not," he said, and kind of smiled, but only kind of.

"Catch you later, Minnesota," Dylan said as he guided Brenda away.

Brenda didn't understand Brandon's problem. She was going out with his friend. *His* friend. Maybe that was the problem. Before, he'd been Brenda's sister and Dylan's friend. Now he had to share both of them. Brandon could be so possessive sometimes.

At dinner, Brenda listened with half an ear while Mrs. Walsh went on and on about how relaxed a couple of her Minneapolis friends were when they returned from a weekend at a spa. Brenda was thinking about Dylan. Mrs. Brenda McKay. Mrs. Brenda McKay-Walsh. Mrs. Brenda Walsh-McKay. Mrs. Dylan McKay.

"What did you say, Dad?" Brenda asked.

"I asked what your plans are for the weekend."

A loaded question if ever there was one. But she could not pussyfoot around forever. As if it were just another date, Brenda said, "I'll probably go out to a movie or something. With Dylan."

Everybody at the table stopped moving. The silence was tense. They were playing a scene straight out of an old western. The hero had just said something the villain didn't like and now the entire saloon was just waiting for the big shoot-out.

"I really don't want you getting involved with him, honey."

Dad's Mr. Reasonable voice. Brenda knew she was in trouble, but she forged ahead. "It's a little late for that Dad," she said.

"What do you mean?" Dad asked.

"What do *you* mean?"

"I mean I don't want you dating him. Period."

Another deafening silence. Brandon did not

appear likely to leap to her aid, so she was in this all by herself. Anything Brenda said would most likely lead to a shouting match between her and her dad. Any such match was bound to be inconclusive. Tomorrow there would be apologies, which would also be inconclusive. The best thing she could do was to avoid the whole situation by agreeing with him. "I see," she said. "Well, then I'll just make plans with Kelly instead."

She carried her dirty dishes to the sink and then hurried upstairs. Behind her, Brenda could hear her parents arguing. "I have a right to my opinion," her dad said.

In her room Brenda just sort of pfumphered around, picking stuff up and setting it down. Dad could be so unreasonable sometimes. It was *her* life. She could go out with whomever she wanted to. Besides, all he knew about Dylan was that his father was some kind of major white-collar crook. He didn't know anything about Dylan himself.

After a while Brenda calmed down enough to actually open her health book to the chapter on nutrition. Dull stuff.

Her mom came up and sat on the bed with her. Brenda hesitated, then turned to her mother and said, "Mom, do you know how it feels in your heart when you finally connect with somebody totally?"

Wistfully, Mom said, "If it's the right person, and the right time, it feels wonderful."

Ready for another argument, Brenda said, "And you agree with Dad? You think Dylan's not the right person?"

"I didn't say that. He's bright. And he's very good-looking." Mom smiled.

Brenda was relieved to find Mom really understood. Brenda said, "Is there a *but* coming?"

Mom thought for a moment and then said, "Brenda, so many things go into a relationship—like mutual respect and commitment.

The front doorbell rang, saving Brenda from whatever homily her mom would deliver next. As she ran from the room she said, "That's Kelly. I'm going to her house to study."

On her way downstairs she met Brandon coming up. "Thanks for your support at the dinner table," she said sarcastically.

"I couldn't claim that Dylan's a Boy Scout. Not even you would believe me."

"Still—"

"Still, after Mom went upstairs, Dad asked me to defend the family honor, to threaten Dylan or something. I told him I wouldn't."

"That's something, I guess. Thanks." She continued downstairs and let Kelly in. "I'm surrounded," Brenda said quietly. "Let's get out of here."

Kelly drove them to her house, and they threw their books on her desk. Brenda explained the situation as she saw it—a terrible conspiracy to prevent her from being happy—and Kelly commiserated. She kept stressing the physical possibilities of Brenda's relationship with Dylan.

Brenda said, "I guess I'm more into the romance angle, like in the movies."

"In real life, romance will never replace sex. At least not for long. You do have protection, don't you?"

"Well, no."

"Basic rule number one: never never trust the guy. Memorize that." She picked up her purse and rummaged in it.

Brenda hugged herself. "God, you sound so clinical."

"Would you rather sit around thinking up names?" Kelly spread the names against the air with one hand. "How about Dylan Junior? Or Brendina?" They both laughed. Kelly cut off the laughter by handing Brenda a couple of square foil packets. Protection. Never trust the guy. Just holding the packets in her hand was embarrassing. But she knew Kelly was right.

4

Brotherly love

ACROSS THE QUAD BRANDON SAW
Brenda and Dylan sitting on the grass beneath
a tree. They ate lunch, casually touched, and
frequently shared laughter. The whole scene
bothered him and he was bothered more
because he didn't know why.

Brandon was confused by his feelings about
Brenda and Dylan. Not separately. Separately,
he still knew how to relate to them. But as a
couple they confused him, and the confusion
frustrated him.

He was older than Brenda by a few minutes, and he was the guy, and he considered it

natural that he feel protective toward his little
sister. Add to that the fact that despite their
friendship, Dylan was still a pretty mysterious
guy. Rumors about him ranged from suspicions
that he frequently ditched school to go surfing,
to whispered speculation about foreign
intrigues with women of dubious repute.

Brandon knew that Dylan liked to surf, but
as for the more outrageous claims, Brandon
himself had once been a victim of the rumor
mill and so was less inclined to believe them.
Still, the word on the street was that the girls
found Dylan to be pretty cute. And his air of
mystery did not hurt his desirability. Would
Brenda fall for the first cute guy who looked at
her twice? She hadn't in Minneapolis, but this
was Beverly Hills. They were different people.
Who knew?

He was preoccupied with this question for
the rest of the day, and when he saw Dylan getting into his car, Brandon ran over to speak
with him. He had no idea what he would say.
But he had to say something or go crazy.

For a while, Brandon just made friendly
conversation. They talked in vague terms about
the weekend. Then Brandon said, "I was thinking maybe we could hit the beach, and then
spend some time under Mondale's hood. My
engine is sounding a little queasy."

"I'd like to, Bran, but my old man is back in

town and he's kind of . . ." Dylan searched for words, made a sound of frustration, and shrugged before he said, "Long story."

"And you don't have time to tell me about it, right?"

Dylan studied him for a moment before saying, "Not really."

Something about Dylan's casual self-assured tone, a tone Brandon had always admired, made him angry. "But you do have time to make out with Brenda," he said. "Or is that just until next month, when you suddenly won't be able to find time for her either?"

Dylan looked around, as if for witnesses, and said, "Where is this coming from?"

"From a concern for Brenda, that's all. You better really like her. She's very romantic, and dreamy, and sweet, and—" What was he trying to say, anyway? "And she's not going to just move on as easily as you will. She's still a virgin, you know."

Dylan stared at him in disbelief. "Brandon, I would not dirty my mind trying to imagine what kind of slime bucket you think I am. Besides, I'm kind of busy right now. Have a nice weekend." He got into his car and roared away, screeching around the first turn, which he took a little too fast.

While he watched, Brandon wondered if anything he'd said to Dylan was true, if any of it even made sense. Maybe not. Yet he felt that Dylan was hiding something. He only hoped it had nothing to do with Brenda.

But something was definitely going on. Their parents would have to be blind not to see it. Friday evening Kelly was over helping Brenda pick out earrings and necklaces and stuff, theoretically for a girls' night out. They were underfoot while he tried to get ready for his big evening working at the Peach Pit.

The fact was, Brenda never glowed from within like that for Kelly, not for any of her girlfriends. Brandon had no doubt that Brenda had a big date with Dylan. Could anything that made Brenda that happy, even for a little while, really be bad?

The next morning Brandon found out that it could. Dad mentioned in passing that Brenda's eyes looked puffy. Brandon had noticed the puffy eyes himself, but had not mentioned it. Sooner or later Brenda would tell him what was going on. She was constitutionally unable to do otherwise. If he pried, she'd never tell him.

Much to Dad's bewilderment Brenda burst into tears at his comment about her eyes and she ran to her room. He looked to Mom for guidance.

"She was obviously in a bad mood. You could have said 'boo' and that would have been enough."

Dad was still looking at the doorway through which Brenda had gone. "I thought she was sleeping at Kelly's."

Bingo, Brandon thought. With his non sequitur Dad was on to something and he probably didn't even know it.

Mom said, "They must have had a fight. She didn't want to talk about it."

I'll bet, Brandon thought. Dylan's fingerprints were all over this ugly mess. Anger rose in him, but he didn't know yet what he would do about it.

"Should I apologize? Maybe I can—"

Brandon interrupted. "Let me talk to her," he said. Dad was a good guy, but sometimes he wasn't very subtle.

Upstairs, Brandon found Brenda on her bed, sniffing and dabbing at her eyes with tissue. When she saw him, Brenda took a deep breath and said evenly, "He didn't show up, Brandon. I was ready to spend the night with him, and he didn't even show up. What a jerk, huh?"

There it was, then. Brandon's second worst fear confirmed. Something needed to be done. An old-fashioned knife fight in a dark alley? A month's detention in study hall? A civilized debate? A strong letter to the *Times*? Brandon's anger still had nowhere to go. At the moment he could only commiserate with Brenda. "He sure can be," he said.

"Not Dylan," Brenda said. "Me!"

"You can't beat yourself up over somebody like him."

"I thought you guys were friends."

"We are. Were. Are. I don't know. I guess there's a lot I don't know about him."

"That's just it," Brenda cried. "He trusted me enough to tell me *everything*."

"Everything?"

Brenda got ahold of herself, though she still seemed upset on Dylan's behalf. "Like that his parents never really wanted kids, and he tries to pretend it's okay, but it *kills* him." She shook her head and began to get weepy again. "I don't understand it. We were *there*. Even just yesterday on the lawn we were together, we were in sync. I don't know what happened." She met Brandon's eyes. "Something happened."

Yeah. What had happened was that Dylan McKay had revealed himself to be an unprincipled clod and he had hurt Brenda bad. Brandon tried to think of something appropriate he could do to Dylan without going to jail for the rest of his life.

"Brandon, I wasn't going to ask you this, but I just feel so bad. Will you talk to him for me?"

Talk? Big knives, firing squads at dawn, premature burial maybe. But talk?

Evidently Brenda mistook Brandon's ruminative silence for unwillingness. "Please," she said. "I need to find out what I did wrong. I need to know what happened."

Brandon said that he would. He needed to know, too. Dylan had hurt Brenda terribly, but he'd also failed Brandon as a friend. He needed to know what was going on as badly as Brenda did.

On Monday Brandon didn't see Dylan till tech class. Dylan was in the corner laboring with a screwdriver over a piece of electronic gear. Brandon came over and watched him for a while. Dylan ignored him, but the tension between them could have been played like a violin string.

"Busy lately, Dylan?" Brandon asked.

Without stopping his work, Dylan said, "Well, if it isn't the master of tact and diplomacy."

"Would you rather talk to Brenda?"

Dylan set down the screwdriver with a bang and turned angrily to Brandon. "Don't start with me again, man. I got the message. You don't want me to hurt your sister."

"So how come that's exactly what you did? Just to spite me?"

As if he were really sorry, Dylan said, "It wasn't because of you, believe me. Something just came up."

"Came up?" Brandon said with astonishment. "I don't mind if you shut me out. But when you do it to her, she feels as if she did something wrong."

"It wasn't her. It had nothing to do with her."

Brandon did not quite poke his finger into Dylan's chest, but he thought about it while he said, "Why don't you tell her that? She was so upset all weekend, she even stayed home from school today."

Dylan said nothing. He just tapped the end of the screwdriver against the table.

With disgust Brandon said, "It had nothing to do with her. It had nothing to do with me. But you're not talking to either one of us. Makes a lot of sense."

Dylan tapped the end of the screwdriver against the table.

After a while Brandon went to work on his own project and tried to lose himself in the physical labor.

Brenda was bored. She still felt awful about the weekend; she wasn't faking that. But she'd watched *Dirty Dancing* twice and had tried to read a little in *The Scarlet Letter*, which even her English teacher called the dullest book ever written about adultery, and now she was just drinking tea. Her mind was blank, which was actually a nice change from what her mind had been serving up lately.

The front doorbell rang, startling her. She

did not feel like leaving the couch, but she was the only one home, so she went to the door and looked through the peephole. On the other side of the door, looking at his shoes, was Dylan. Brenda felt an extraordinary combination of exaltation and rage. She straightened the oversized shirt she was wearing, pulled up her blue leggings, and opened the door.

Dylan smiled at her. She did not smile back.

Dylan said, "I'm not real good at this."

That's for certain, Brenda thought. She was not about to help him do whatever he'd come here to do.

Dylan said, "I'm sorry. I feel terrible."

Ha, thought Brenda.

"I don't know what else to say."

"You might start with why you stood me up Friday night."

Dylan peered at a space over Brenda's left shoulder. He looked genuinely apologetic, but Brenda was determined not to fall for whatever line he was throwing her. Then he began to speak and her resolve melted away.

Dylan said, "Brenda, I didn't meet you on Friday because I had to help my father pack. He found out he's going to be indicted. Securities fraud. Something like that. He needed to disappear."

"Oh, Dylan," Brenda said tenderly, and put a hand on his arm.

"I kept thinking about you the whole time. But I had to do this for my father. Please don't think I didn't care. I did. I do."

"I wish you would have called me."

"I just couldn't."

"*I* called *you*."

"When? Nobody told me."

"Now I feel terrible." It was true. Brenda had no way of knowing whether Dylan was telling the truth or not, but her intuition told her that he was. They could not have been so good together if Dylan was not basically a good person, as she was.

Dylan looked into her eyes. "Please don't. I don't want you to feel terrible anymore." He cupped her face in his hands and kissed her very gently.

After that, they somehow were embracing. And somehow they made their way to the couch. And somehow the kissing continued and only got better. Brenda loved Dylan. She was certain of it. One could not feel this way and not be in love.

At the same moment, they both heard a car pulling into the driveway, and they sprang apart as if they'd been tugged by ropes.

Brenda ran to look out the window. Shocked by what she saw, she turned to Dylan. "It's my father. Come on."

She ran to the kitchen and Dylan followed.

They draped themselves around the kitchen table and tried to look casual. A second later, Dad came through the kitchen door with a newspaper in one hand and a weary expression on his face. He looked at the two of them with disbelief.

"Hi, Dad. Remember Dylan?"

"I was just leaving. Nice to see you again, sir." Dylan stood and headed for the door with an exaggerated languor while her father watched the performance with increasing anger and incredulity.

"I'll tell Brandon you came by," Brenda said sincerely.

When Dylan was out the door, Dad said, "What kind of idiot do you take me for, Brenda?"

You're not an idiot, Brenda thought. And I'm doomed.

5

Slack

BRENDA WONDERED WHAT LIFE IN A convent would be like. Certainly, Dad intended to do worse than ground her. Sending her to live in a convent seemed about right. She would carry Dylan forever in her heart, her one real, eternal love. She would—

"You want to learn about your pal Dylan?" her dad said, and threw the newspaper onto the table. On the front page was a headline about Jack McKay. Dad went on, "His father's exploits would make a great novel. Maybe he can write it in prison."

So what Dylan had told her was true. That

made her feel better. But the story about his father was terrible. She asked, "Was he arrested?"

"Not yet." This fact seemed to inflame her dad. "He skipped town. Some role model, huh? Some example."

Brenda was amazed by her dad's attitude. "Dad, Dylan is nothing like his father."

"Well," said Dad, backpedaling quickly, "you deserve better."

"Like who? Somebody straighter? Younger? Quieter?"

"For a start."

"Dad, those 'nice' boys may be mild-mannered on the outside, but mostly what they think about is sex."

"Who said anything about sex?" Dad hung his coat over the back of a chair and loosened his tie. "I'm talking about a person's values, his character—"

Brenda looked her father in the eye and let him have it. "Why is it with Brandon you just made sure he knew about birth control, but my entire value system is on the line here?"

Dad shrugged. Brenda knew by his body language that she had him good. The crisis was over. "It's different for a girl," he said. "It just is. You need to know who you're dealing with."

"What do you want me to say? That I'll wait till I get married?" Dad looked so whipped that she actually took pity on him. He was stuck in

one of those old-fashioned middle-class morali-
ty paradoxes. Brenda said, "You look so disappointed. And I haven't even done anything!"

Dad sat down and took her hand. "I'm not
disappointed. I just don't know that I'm ready
to—I mean that *you're* ready to . . ."

They just looked at each other for a
moment. Brenda knew that her dad loved her,
and no matter what happened she would
always be Daddy's little girl. Which, unfortu-
nately, was part of the problem. She squeezed
his hand and said, "And if I'm ready first, Dad?
Then what? Should I lie and sneak around? Or
will you trust me to know what I'm doing?"

Brenda could see by the look on his face
that this was a serious question for her father,
and one not easily answered.

Steve Sanders was walking across campus
after school when he saw Mr. Kravitz staring
glumly at his automobile. The hood was up.
The car would not start and he had to wait for a
tow truck. Why today of all days, when he had
to pick up the guest speaker for the sex-educa-
tion assembly they were having the next day?
For some reason, Steve volunteered to go to
the airport for him. Mr. Kravitz hesitated only a
moment before he agreed.

Mr. Kravitz said, "Palm West Air from

Chicago. Stacy Sloan. Bel Age Hotel. Don't screw this up."

"No problem, Mr. K. But you'll owe me one." Steve ran for his car.

At the airport, Steve made contact with Ms. Sloan and knew he'd struck a major vein of luck. She was a willowy blonde who dressed well, if a little conservatively, and had a nice personality. Somehow she had acquired the idea that Steve was Mr. Kravitz, and Steve did nothing to correct her. This misconception could be very advantageous to him.

After Steve had helped Ms. Sloan carry her bags up to her room at the Bel Age, Steve asked, "So, what time shall I pick you up tonight?"

But Ms. Sloan refused to be bullied, bull-dozed, or flattered into seeing Steve that evening. She was gentle but firm. Steve bowed, and kissed her hand before departing.

When Brandon heard about Brenda's discussion with their dad, he was impressed. More than that, it gave him something else to think about. Obviously, the relationship between Brenda and Dylan involved more than a fast game of touchy-feely. Despite appearances, it could not always be easy to be Dylan McKay. Brandon decided to cut him a lot of slack.

Evidently, their dad was ready to do the

same. He backed off from his demand that Dylan never darken his door again, and left open the question of Brenda dating him.

Brandon went to the auditorium with the rest of the kids who were taking health and had managed to wangle a signed parental-consent form. He stood in the cool dimness against the back wall watching kids mill around.

Steve Sanders was exercising his charm on a group of girls. Steve was a wild man. He'd actually convinced Stacy Sloan that he was Mr. Kravitz. Ms. Sloan and the real Mr. Kravitz were on stage talking and looking in Steve's direction. When Steve noticed, he broke away from the girls and went to the back of the auditorium, where he slouched in a chair directly in front on Brandon.

"I don't want to hear about it," Steve grumbled.

"Is this space taken?"

Brandon was surprised to see Dylan standing next to him, waiting for permission to lean against the wall. He shrugged at Dylan's question and moved down the wall to give him room. Despite his decision to cut Dylan slack, Brandon discovered that he still held some residual anger. Things might have been straight between Dylan and Brenda, but he and Brandon still had unfinished business. They both leaned against the wall, arms folded, watching the stage.

"So," said Dylan, "if you still need help with your car, I could do it this weekend."

"It's okay. I can handle it." Brandon sounded stiffer than he wanted to be. He told himself to lighten up.

Dylan shook his head. "Somehow I'm always apologizing to you Walshes. I'm sorry if you felt like I checked out on you."

"I guess that bothered me more than I thought. I'm sorry I opened my big mouth about Brenda."

"Would you have felt better if I'd asked you first—about seeing her, I mean?"

Who knew? Brandon certainly didn't know. Probably, if Dylan had asked permission to date his sister, Brandon would have said something like, "Why ask me? Why don't you ask Brenda?" Which is exactly what Dylan had done. Brandon wondered if *he* was the jerk here.

Brandon shrugged again, but it was a friendlier shrug than the first one, and it came with a smile. He and Dylan shook hands and found seats in the last row behind Steve.

The crowd grew quiet when Andrea Zuckerman stepped to the lectern to introduce the guest speaker, Stacy Sloan. While not as spectacularly beautiful as some of the other girls at West Beverly, Andrea was not without

her charm. She had an open intelligent face
and long, curly hair. She was also Brandon's
boss, the editor of the school paper. Neither of
them could decide if their relationship was just
a friendship or something more.

Ms. Sloan came forward and there was the
predictable polite applause. Steve had not lied.
Stacy Sloan was quite a dish.

Steve whispered over his shoulder to
Brandon, "Not bad, eh? Bel Age Hotel. Room
316."

Steve was incorrigible.

Ms. Sloan hesitated then spoke quietly but
firmly. "I had an experience just after I arrived
here I'd like to share with you. A young man
wanted to show me around town. 'Get to know
me better.'"

Ms. Sloan's knowing delivery caused
almost everyone to laugh.

"Well, the timing wasn't right, and I told
him that."

Brandon knew who Ms. Sloan was talking
about. He leaned over the seat and grabbed
Steve's shoulder. "Way to go, champ." Steve
sank lower in his chair.

"It was a shame, too. He was very handsome. For one thing he had these incredible
blue eyes."

More laughter as the members of the audience appreciated Ms. Sloan's predicament.

Steve sat up a little straighter.

More slowly Ms. Sloan said, "What I didn't tell him is what I'm going to have to tell every guy who's interested in me for the rest of my life: I have AIDS."

It was a moment the likes of which no horror movie could ever duplicate. For inducing fear and loathing, Freddy Krueger had nothing on AIDS. Brandon had never heard a crowd so silent. He could hear Dylan breathing. He imagined he could hear his own heart beating. Steve sat up in his chair and leaned forward. Brandon could imagine the expression of surprise on his face, the feeling of having barely escaped a death sentence.

Ms. Sloan went on to tell her story. About how she'd had her first sexual experience with a lawyer when she was sixteen. How she'd found out years later that he'd died of AIDS. She had tests done and found that she had it, too, evidently had had it for some time.

Then she cautioned her rapt audience about who they had sex with, and how they had sex. The message hit home with the force of a knock from a baseball bat. It made an impression the way all the classroom discussions and dire warnings from parents never could.

When she was done, the kids gave Ms. Sloan a standing ovation, a recognition of her bravery, of their sorrow at her plight, and maybe as a little magic to ward off the same thing happening to them. In any case the applause was sincere, and went on long after she'd returned to her seat. When the kids filed out, they did it quietly, as if leaving a funeral.

Brandon, Dylan, and Steve were on their way out of the auditorium when Steve stopped. Ms. Sloan was talking near the stage to a group of earnest kids. She saw Steve and came over to him. "I hope I didn't get you into hot water," she said.

Steve shook his head and, with some disgust, said, "No. I can do that fine by myself. Ms. Sloan, I'm sorry. I hope I didn't—I don't know what I'm trying to say."

"Tell me you heard what I was trying to get across here today and I'll go home happy."

Brandon had never seen Steve so serious. The man obviously had depths and feelings that Brandon had never given him credit for. Steve said, "I heard you. And my offer for dinner stands. Call me next time you're in town."

Ms. Sloan hugged him and Steve hugged back. For the first time Brandon had the feeling that Steve was hugging to give and get comfort, not for sex. They separated, and the real Mr. Kravitz guided Ms. Sloan away.

As they left the auditorium Dylan said to Steve, "Very classy, man."

"Yeah, well."

Brandon could see that Steve wanted to say something flippant, but he didn't. Steve just said, "Don't let it get around that inside the slick operator is mashed bananas. Okay?"

Brenda heard the doorbell ring downstairs and knew it would be Dylan. She looked at herself again in the mirror, gave her hair another brush, adjusted the collar of her shirt. Were the earrings too dangly? Too late to change now. If he really loved her, maybe the earrings wouldn't matter.

Mom came into her room and said, "Dylan's here."

"Thanks, Mom."

They were halfway down the stairs when they heard the voices in the living room. Mom put her hand on Brenda's arm and they stopped to listen.

"So, Dylan," Dad said, "how are you holding up?"

Brenda thought her dad sounded a little nervous, as if he were trying hard to be friendly but was not yet comfortable with it. Brenda would settle for nervousness any day over the unreasonable anger her dad had dished out before.

"I'm okay. I just don't talk to the press." Dylan sounded fine, ready to make peace, sincerely answering a sincere question. "I've always felt odd being known as 'Jack McKay's son.' After all, I hardly known the man."

"That's a shame when that happens."

"Yeah. Brandon and Brenda are very lucky to have parents like you."

Brenda felt like crying, but she couldn't allow herself the luxury. Her makeup would run and her eyes would get puffy. To save herself from this embarrassment, she made a lot of noise descending the stairs and found Dylan and her dad just standing in the middle of the living room. Dylan joined her. She hugged her father. When they parted, Dad didn't know what to do with hands. He looked a little weepy, too. "You take care now," he said softly as they went into the night.

Still Daddy's little girl, Brenda thought. But maybe not quite so little anymore. One small step . . .

The wind blew in Brenda's hair as Dylan drove his Porsche up into the Hollywood Hills. She felt very dreamy and romantic and she gave herself up to the feelings. Dylan turned onto Mulholland and they drove along the spine of the range, allowing them to glimpse the lights of the valley on one side and then of Los Angeles on the other.

Dylan pulled over at a turnout and stopped

the engine. The spicy smell of Southern California shrubs came to Brenda on the cool air. Below, the grids of Beverly Hills and West Hollywood were laid out in tiny lights. For a while Brenda and Dylan did not even touch each other; they just watched the lights. The waiting, the tension, was delicious. Brenda knew they had not come up here to study geography.

Playfully, Brenda asked, "What I want to know, Dylan, is how many times you've come up here to park." She leaned toward him a little, her lips slightly parted, as Kelly had suggested.

"I come up here a lot. I like the view." Dylan leaned forward, too. They were almost touching.

"You come up here alone?" Brenda whispered.

"Sometimes."

They kissed, and it was even better than before. She had parental approval. Hell, she had her own approval, which was even more important. Dylan was no longer just the most mysterious guy at school. He was her boyfriend and her friend.

They were all over each other. Brenda regretted that Dylan's very hip car was so small. One of those gangster coupes was about right for what she had in mind. No, no. Her emotions were getting away from her. She gently pushed Dylan back to his side of the car and said, "Dylan, I have to ask you something."

"Ask away." He moved toward her again and nibbled her ear, which under normal circumstances would have made her crazy, but she had serious business and she held on to herself.

Brenda said, "Don't get mad, okay?"

He worked his way down the side of her neck. "I never get mad." Now her other ear.

"Listen, Dylan. Did you ever have sex? I mean, did you ever have sex when you weren't protected?"

"Not lately," Dylan breathed into her ear.

This wasn't working. She couldn't concentrate. Brenda held Dylan's face in both her hands. His eyebrows went up. He made that wonderful quirky smile. He waited. Brenda asked again, "Did you ever have sex when you weren't protected?"

Dylan relaxed against his door. "Well, yeah."

"Oh." This was terrible, but she could handle it. After all, they had more than sex going for them. Still, she liked to think that all was not lost.

"You worried about that?" Dylan asked.

Brenda twisted her hands together. This could blow the whole deal or make it. "I guess I'm assuming that you want to with me . . ."

Dylan watched her. He did not seem to be angry; Brenda could not tell what his attitude was.

"Am I blowing this totally? Am I thinking

too much?"

"I like people that think, Brenda. So what are you saying? You want me to get a test?"

Brenda began to sniffle and tear up. Living in the nineties was so difficult. Dylan found a tissue in his glove compartment and gave it to her. While sopping up the tears, she said, "I'm not used to these feelings, and I want to be sure. And I'm scared, not just of the disease, but that you'll say no." She took a deep ragged breath.

"I'm not saying no."

"You're not?" She was surprised at her own surprise. If Dylan was the guy she thought he was, of course he would not say no. She felt relieved and very happy. Maybe this would work out after all.

"No. I said yes."

They moved toward each other again and sealed Dylan's agreement with a kiss. A long kiss with all the trimmings. It lasted a few hours, not counting the occasional surfacing for air when they actually admired the view, and Brenda knew this was love.

Even the harsh reality of driving to school with Brandon on Monday morning could not entirely sweep away the floaty feeling inside Brenda. It actually lasted through most of the week. The misunderstanding she had had with Dylan seemed to have drawn them even closer together. They ate lunch together, and often Dylan drove her home. She felt appreciated and happy. Dylan was nearly adopted by the Walshes, which he seemed to enjoy.

Aside from the fact of school itself, only driving to school with Brandon was kind of a drag. Most of the time, Brandon was a careful driver, but the fact was, they were traveling in Mondale—a car that was almost ten years old, and had not been very stylish when it was new. Brandon was less bummed than Brenda by Mondale. He claimed the engine was pristine, and that's what counted. Brenda knew nothing about pristine engines and didn't care to learn either.

On their way to school on Friday, Brandon and Brenda discussed their plans for the weekend and came up dry. Dylan was going to Baja for the surfing, leaving Brenda pretty much on her own. Brandon had only the Peach Pit to look forward to, and that only if Nat called him in.

"I get bored just thinking about the rut my life is in," Brandon confessed.

"Yeah," said Brenda.

"Yeah, what? You are dating the coolest dude in school. Your life is one big round of adventure and romance. All I have to look forward to is the opportunity to fine-tune my engine and serve burgers to the hungry masses." He stopped for a red light.

"What would you like to do, Brandon?"

"Something else."

Brenda smiled and, to tease him, said, "With anyone I know?"

Brandon considered that before he said, "No. With a total stranger. Maybe one who looks like Kim Basinger."

As they waited for the light to turn, Steve pulled up next to them in his black Corvette. Brenda knew that Steve was stuck up about his car so she tried not to appear impressed. Steve made rude remarks about Mondale, and Brandon valiantly defended Mondale's honor. Steve shrugged and laughed. Riled by Steve's comments, Brandon claimed Mondale could beat the black Corvette to school.

Brenda was suddenly afraid. Why did guys have to do stuff like this? "Don't do anything stupid, Brandon," she said. "Personally, I'd like to make it to first period in one piece."

"No problem-o, Bren. Mario Andretti has nothing on me." He gunned his engine. Next to them, Steve was gunning the 'vette. While waiting for the green light, Brenda clutched the dashboard and tried to remember prayers she'd last said many years before in Sunday school.

6

The designated mom

THE LIGHT TURNED GREEN, THE ENGINES
roared, and a split second later Brenda was
thrown forward against her seat belt. A police
car turned smoothly onto the street in front of
them. Brandon swore and looked over at
Steve, who smiled sweetly and motioned him to
go first.

"Answered prayers," Brenda said, and half
believed it.

Brandon shook his head and smiled rueful-
ly. "No, Bren, it's all part of the pattern of my
life. I'm doomed to grow old without my system ever again feeling a shot of adrenaline."

Brandon was in a wild and reckless mood. He could not sit still. He threatened to join the Foreign Legion. Brenda thought that if he did not succeed in killing himself in the next week or so, he would probably live, with or without an adrenaline rush.

At school, as everyone hurried to classes, Donna announced that she was throwing an impromptu party that evening. "Very intimate," she said. "Strictly A list."

"What will your parents say?" Brenda asked.

Donna smiled with secret pleasure. "They left this morning for Cabo San Lucas," she said offhandedly.

"It's a Beverly Hills tradition," Kelly explained. "When your parents leave town, you must throw a party."

"Can I invite Dylan?"

Kelly looked at Brenda and said, "Sure, if you want to live dangerously."

Brenda burned and quickly made her escape around the corner, and, as it happened, ran straight into Dylan. They smiled at each other. Brenda felt the surge of expectation and warmth she always felt when she saw him. She said, "Donna's having a party tonight. Strictly A list. I don't suppose you'd give up your surfing plans to escort me."

"I really hate parties. Especially A-list parties.

Why don't you come with me to Baja?"

Brenda was alarmed by Dylan's question, and then was relieved when he admitted he wasn't serious. Unless *she* was. Brenda sighed. "Maybe another time," she said. She didn't know if she was ready for a trip to Baja with Dylan. She knew her dad wasn't.

"I'll make it up to you next weekend," Dylan said.

"Sounds like a date to me."

That took care of next weekend. But this evening would be a problem. On the drive home from school, Brenda was very quiet, looking for a way out of her predicament. Brandon didn't notice. He was busy singing the theme from *Raiders of the Lost Ark* over and over again while he kept time against the steering wheel.

After they got home, Brenda decided that she really had no way out. She went into Brandon's room and found him making whooshing noises and throwing paper airplanes across the room. He had an entire fleet of airplanes on his bed with him and many more on the floor around the wastebasket. She asked him nicely if he would take her to Donna's party, and without even stopping his launching, he firmly said no.

"I don't want to go to this party alone."

Brandon threw another plane. "All right. I'll

drive you. But I refuse to go in."

"You have to go in. Just this morning you complained that your life is in a rut and totally boring. Here's your big chance to break out."

Brandon glanced at Brenda and took another shot. "I'm just not good at parties."

Desperate situations called for desperate measures. Brenda put her arms around Brandon's neck and kissed him across the top of his head. "Please, Brandon? Pretty please with motor oil on it?"

He struggled from her grasp. "Hey, save it for tonight."

"You see," said Brenda. "I need you there to protect me from stuff like that."

"I'll think about it."

Brenda kissed him again and left the room before she said too much. She knew Brandon. Once he promised to think about something, he was doomed.

At dinner, Mom and Dad announced that they were going away the following weekend. "To my corporate retreat." He looked at Mom moony-eyed and said, "This year it's in Santa Barbara."

"I want to go," Brenda said. Santa Barbara was a small town about two hours up the coast from Los Angeles. It could be very romantic. She knew her chances of actually going were nil, but she felt she should show some interest.

"Sorry," said Dad. "It's strictly adults only."

"All sounds pretty rooty-tooty to me," Brandon commented.

Suddenly serious, Mom said, "Would you two be terribly disappointed if we skipped town and left you alone?"

"No problem-o," Brandon said.

Why did Brandon have to be such a child? He could blow this entire thing.

Mom said, "Seriously, your father and I feel that you are old enough now to take care of yourselves for a few days."

As maturely as she could, Brenda said, "Thank you, Mother. We will try to be true to your trust." She prayed her parents couldn't see how fast her heart was beating as she smiled serenely at them.

Brandon really hated big parties. He hated the noise, the social pressures, the fact that usually he found nobody he wanted to talk to. He was no good at small talk. Give him big talk every time.

Still, Brenda was right about his being in a rut. A party might be just the thing to drag him out of it, screaming and kicking.

Donna's house was the usual Beverly Hills mausoleum. Light showed in every window, and he could hear the music half a block away.

Already, Brandon felt uncomfortable.

Brenda, dressed casually, but very much the party dudette, said, "You must come in with me, Brandon," and he bowed to the inevitable.

Donna let them into the house, and Brandon saw that the A list consisted mainly of the people he'd expected—Donna's friends. Most of them were gathered around the wet bar in the corner of the living room. The only one Brandon hadn't actually met was Drew, Donna's current squeeze. He was a big hunk of a guy cut from the same cloth as Steve Sanders, but not as bright. He was the kind of guy who always tied the arms of his sweater around his neck instead of actually wearing the sweater.

Everybody at the bar was watching Steve as if he were performing magic. Actually, all he was doing was mixing ice and alcohol and flavorings in a blender, but he made a production out of it. He stopped the blender, announced, "Mucho marvelous margaritas," and filled glasses with slushy greenish stuff.

Kelly tasted hers and said, "They're too good, Brenda."

"I didn't know you drank."

"My mom drinks. I sip." Kelly saw that Brenda was unconvinced and went on, "It's a lot easier than saying no." Kelly smiled and wriggled her shoulders. "And you get a little loose." She handed the drink to Brenda.

Brenda took a sip and smiled broadly.

Brandon had a bad feeling about this party. He was no monk, but ever since he'd had a disgusting experience with a can of beer at the age of fifteen he'd been leery of drinking. He tried not to let it bother him, and he tried not to impose his feelings on anybody else. Except for Brenda, maybe; his attempts with her rarely worked anyway.

Steve thrust an icy glass into Brandon's hand and told him to drink up. Brandon set the glass on the bar and asked for a cola.

Steve blinked and stared at him in disbelief. Drew shook his head. Brenda covered her face with one hand. The others merely chuckled. "You want soda pop?" Steve asked.

Kelly said, "Leave him alone, Steve. He doesn't want to drink. Big deal."

Drew smirked and leaned toward Steve. "I think Brandon's afraid of the wild man lurking inside him."

"I just don't like the taste," Brandon said.

"Me neither," Steve said. "At least let me make you a virgin margarita."

Brandon shrugged. "Whatever."

He was pulled into a conversation with Donna, Drew, and Kelly about awful teachers and who was seeing who—the usual gab. The talk was very small, but Brandon found that he was enjoying himself more than he expected. In any case the view of Los Angeles out the picture window was awesome. Steve brought him a virgin margarita and presented it with a small bow.

Soon the lights went down. Slow dancing only a step from heavy necking began, and sometimes it was only half a step. Brandon carried his virgin margarita onto the deck out back for some air, and to take in the view. At night the air in L.A. wasn't so bad actually. It was a little on the cool side, but not as cool as it would have been at this time of year back east. And the brush growing on the hillside perfumed the air with heady smells unknown in Minnesota. He took a deep breath. As sort of an exercise he tried to describe the scene in words, but the words seemed slippery tonight.

Brenda appeared beside him with a half-full margarita glass in her hand. A little miffed, she asked him what he was doing out here all by himself. "Feena Farris has been watching you like a hungry animal all evening."

"She eyes everybody like a hungry animal." They watched the lights of Los Angeles twinkle under the cloud cover. Stars below but not above. Odd. Brandon knew he would have to ask Brenda the big question sooner or later. He didn't enjoy being the responsible one, but somebody had to do it. He asked, "Brenda, how many drinks have you had?"

"This is my second, *'Mom.'* Why don't you have one?"

"Because I'm the designated mom. Half an hour, Bren."

"All right, Brandon, a half hour. Just do me a favor. Just *try* to loosen up a little. For me? Please?"

"You didn't say 'pretty please with motor oil on top.'"

"I would if I thought it would do any good." She shook her head and went back inside.

A few minutes later Brandon had had enough air and wanted to go inside, too. His feet seemed farther away than usual, and he had to think about controlling them. Well, it had been a long day, a long week. It was late. He hated parties. Why did Brenda do this to him? How could twins be so different? One of them had to be adopted—an alien changeling from Mars, maybe. The thought made him laugh out loud. He'd have to share this.

Brenda didn't think much of the changeling theory and Kelly thought it was just weird, but Donna really got into it and invented a romantic tale of interplanetary lust that made everybody laugh. When Steve came by to refill his glass, Brandon asked, "That's the virgin batch, right, Steve?"

Steve's face was impassive. "Same as last time," he said, and then a laugh exploded from him.

"What? What's so funny?"

Nearby, Drew, who still could not find the neck of his sweater, was laughing uncontrollably.

Brandon knew he'd been had. Those jerks. He said, "You spiked my drink, didn't you, Steve?"

There must have been something about his tone. Conversation around him stopped.

As if explaining the facts of life, Steve said, "We just wanted you to have a good time, Brandon."

Brandon did have a wild man inside him, and everybody was about to see it. He was suddenly very angry. "I think it's up to me how I chose to have a good time," he said. "Let's blow this Popsicle stand, Brenda." Did he mean it? For some reason he was still holding the fatal drink.

"Look, man," said Steve, "it was a bad joke."

"Let him go," Drew said with disgust. "He's ruining the party."

"Brandon, look, I'm sorry. Okay?"

Donna asked him to stay. They all did. It was embarrassing. Maybe he was making a big deal over nothing—a few ounces of alcohol, after all. And this had to be hard on Brenda, her brother wussing out in front of all her friends. Drew said nothing, but he wore an expression of smug superiority. Dumber than compost, Brandon thought.

"I'll get you a soda," Steve said.

Into the long silence that followed, Brandon finally dropped, "No. This is okay. Really." He lifted his glass and drained it all at once. "Cold," he said, and smiled.

Applause began. Steve called him a party machine and Drew called for more margaritas. The gathering was a party again, and Brandon was its brightest star. Brenda gave him the thumbs-up.

7

A Beverly Hills tradition

THIS IS ONE BITCHIN' PARTY, BRANDON thought. I may never go home.

As it turned out Steve really did make a great margarita. Brandon lost count of how many he'd quaffed. Kelly and Steve seemed to have settled their differences and had gone off someplace to be alone. And Brandon himself had the entire attention of Feena Farris, an attention that could start fires if one played one's cards right.

Slowly, the party ran down. Feena Farris's body made big promises to Brandon as they danced, but she left without even giving him her phone number. The crowd thinned. The blender was silent. Brenda and Brandon sprawled on a couch across from Donna and Drew, who seemed fascinated with each other's eyes.

Brandon was not exactly brain dead, but he was very relaxed, and he found even blinking to be an Olympic event. After a while he was aware that he'd been sitting on that couch for a very long time. He found a bathroom, used it, and then took himself and Brenda home.

Knowing he had a couple of drinks in him, Brandon drove slowly. The brakes seemed a little overresponsive and tended to stop the car too fast. Have to look into that. Brenda told him more than he ever wanted to know about Drew, and by the time Mondale bounced up the driveway she and Brandon were both laughing uncontrollably.

They got out of the car still laughing when a thought struck Brandon. He shook Brenda's arm and said, "Straighten up, Bren. Mom'll be on the couch."

"Right, right, right. She'll be pretending to read the same book she's had since we were in the eighth grade." She started to giggle.

Brandon put his finger to his lips and Brenda did the same. He got the door open and they carefully entered the house. As predicted, Mom was on the couch. They told her they'd had a good time, Brenda hugged her good night, and everybody went to bed.

The next morning Brandon tried to balance his head so it wouldn't fall off while he put on his socks. Shouting came from the kitchen—his parents and Brenda. It could be about anything. But Brandon had a feeling they were arguing about alcohol and coming home late from parties. How had Mom and Dad found out?

He sat on his bed for a few minutes and at last decided to go down and give Brenda some support, if she needed it. Maybe he was wrong. Maybe they were arguing about homework. Or maybe Dad had had another paranoid delusion about Dylan. On his way down the stairs he met Brenda on her way up. She was tearful, and full of spite.

"What?" Brandon asked.

"Mom smelled liquor on my breath when we came in last night. Now she and Dad are on the warpath. They'll probably never let me go to a party again."

"You didn't tell them about me?"

"No, Brandon, I didn't. You owe me one. A big one."

Brandon was sorry about Brenda, but he was relieved to hear that he was still clean. He nodded as Brenda ran up the stairs, probably to report to Kelly. He owed Brenda one, but that particular hurdle was in the future. The far future, if he was lucky.

Brandon found his parents sitting at the kitchen table, ready for tennis. Their rackets leaned against the backdoor. "Brenda seems pretty upset," he said.

"You both know the rules, Brandon," Mom said.

"I probably should have said something when she took that first sip, but I didn't think it would do any good." Oh boy, Saint Brandon.

Dad said, "When we're out of town next weekend, we really need you to keep better tabs on your sister."

"I'll do my best, Dad." Brandon wondered who would keep tabs on Brenda's brother. No wonder Brenda was upset. She'd taken the heat for both of them.

Brandon and his parents reassured each other some more, and then they went out to play tennis. Tennis was really a simple game compared with the life of a teenager.

Brenda knew that *she* was really the responsible one, but while her parents were loading the car for the journey to the retreat, Dad said, "Brandon, look out for your sister, okay?"

Brenda couldn't stand it anymore. "Excuse me," she said, "but I think you should be asking *me* to look out for *him*."

"How about you look out for each other?" Mom said.

After Mom and Dad were gone at last, after the car had turned the corner and was out of sight, Brenda gave her brother a dirty look and went back into the house.

The drive to school was a long cool affair, mostly because Brenda was trying to think up a suitable way that Brandon could pay her back for her silence. Nothing much came to her, but it would.

At school Kelly mostly complained about how Steve had taken advantage of her at Donna's party, and how for that reason alone she would never again allow alcohol to pass her lips. When Brenda mentioned in passing that her parents would be out of town through the weekend, the subject changed immediately.

All eagerness, Kelly asked, "What time should we tell people to arrive?"

"I wish," Brenda said, wishing.

"You're not having a party?" Donna asked, amazed.

"I have this problem. He's about my age and his name begins with a *B*."

Kelly offered to work on Brandon, but Brenda turned her down. She wanted to try first herself. Maybe he could pay her back sooner than either of them had imagined.

That evening they decided that they would

rather eat bologna sandwiches than frozen dinners. Brenda waited for just the exact correct moment to spring the party idea on Brandon, then finally decided that none existed. "Did I mention we're having a party here this weekend?" She smiled innocently at Brandon.

"Forget it. What if Mom and Dad find out?"

"They won't. We'll clean up everything before they get home. Besides, I already told Kelly to spread the word." There. She had done it and she was glad.

"Well, tell her to un-spread it." Brandon savagely took another bite out of his sandwich and glared at his sister.

"Brandon, it's our *turn*," Brenda explained as if she were explaining ice to a forgetful Eskimo. This was so obvious. And it was bogus that she had to plead with him anyway. He was only her brother. "Throwing a party when your parents go out of town is practically a tradition in Beverly Hills," she said. "It puts you on the map."

Brandon wasn't even looking at her. He was engrossed in applying more mustard to his bread.

She continued in a more conciliatory tone. "You're worried about people drinking, aren't you?"

"It crossed my mind," he said without looking up.

"Nobody said *we* have to drink."

No response from Brandon.

Time to bring up the big guns. "Besides," Brenda said, "you owe me one."

Brandon looked at her with his big, sad eyes—the eyes of a trapped animal. But he refused to fall over. He said nothing.

Brenda would have to give him one more push just to finish the job. Carefully, she asked, "Brandon, don't you ever get tired of always doing the right thing? Isn't it a strain?"

Brenda could see it in his eyes, the decision to cut loose, to party-down, to let somebody else be the responsible one for a change. When he shouted, "Yes!" Brenda felt that it was an anticlimax.

However, Brandon could not help being a little responsible even then. He was compulsive about it. He made her promise that it would be an A-list party like Donna's, though Donna didn't have to bring Drew if she didn't want to, and they would have no more than twenty-five guests.

Brenda was so jazzed they were going to have a party at all that she agreed to everything. Big parties were a drag, anyway. Who wanted to have a lot of strangers in the house?

On Friday night Brenda spent some time considering what she might wear to her own shindig. She'd probably end up carrying trays of food and dirty glasses, so she shouldn't wear anything too weird or confining or flouncy. Who knew what might spill? She put on a crisp shirt and the jeans that fit her best at the moment. Shoes were as practical as she could stand— very low heels. Very nice. Casual but not grotty.

Brandon looked nice, too, in his straight-ahead, understated way.

In the kitchen they decided on a plan of attack. Drinks in the fridge (soda pop only). Big bags of chips on the counter near the sour cream for dips. Paper cups on the kitchen table—not very fancy but great for cleanup.

They put out chips in the same big wooden bowls their mom used. Brenda looked at all the chips, thought of the twenty-five people who would be there that night, and wondered if maybe they'd gotten a little carried away at the store. "Should I put out the whole bag?"

Brandon said, "Might as well. Seven-year locusts have nothing on our friends. By the way, Bren, how many on the final guest list? Not many, right?"

"Did you ask anybody?"

"Just Andrea. She's going to some New York comedy at the Music Center, but she said she'd be over after."

"I invited Dylan, but he hates parties."

"My man. Who else? So far we have a guest who will arrive late and a no-show. Who's going to eat all this food?"

"Kelly said she asked nine or ten, and I asked six, not counting Dylan." She smiled for him. "Not too many."

"Perfect."

Just before eight, when the party was supposed to start, Brenda took a last look at the living room. Everything in order. Everything under control. The party scene was a total work of art.

There was nothing to do now but wait. She haunted the living room, touching this, straightening that. The book Mom and Dad pretended to read when they waited up was on the coffee table. She opened it, saw that it was dedicated to Jack Enyart, and wondered if he was the same guy who owned the fancy restaurant.

At five after eight, Brenda was convinced that nobody was coming. At ten after eight, Kelly arrived. Donna arrived shortly after, schlepping Drew. Steve showed up around eight-thirty carrying a large mysterious shopping bag that did not remain mysterious for long. From it, he pulled a blender and everything else he needed to make mucho marvelous margaritas. Everything except ice.

"I thought this was going to be a dry party," Brandon said.

"No, Brandon," said Brenda patiently. "I said that *we* did not have to drink."

People continued to arrive. Brenda got busy in the kitchen and left Kelly and Donna to answer the door. Soon she lost track of who was there, or even how many were there. An awful lot of noise seemed to be coming from the living room. There seemed to be twenty-five people just in the kitchen. Many of them were offering drinks from slim brown bottles.

Brenda sighed as she stirred the onion dip. She couldn't stop them from drinking alcohol. If she did, word would get out that she was some kind of a prude. She hadn't had any, and she didn't think Brandon had either. That's what counted.

Brandon managed to squeeze into the kitchen and waved at Brenda. She waved back. He shook his head and hollered something at her. She heard words but could not make them out. They each did that funny sideways dance people use when making their way through crowds, and met at last in front of the stove.

"Do you know any of these people?" Brenda asked. She had to talk right into Brandon's ear.

Brandon said nothing, but crooked his finger at her. She had enough on her mind without Brandon acting like a spy. But she followed him across the dining room and into the foyer. People were lounging against the open front door. With a wave of one hand he invited her to look into the living room.

In one corner couples were dancing in a space barely large enough to stand in. In another Steve was whipping up mucho marvelous margaritas and handing them around in *her* paper cups. In between, Brenda could not see the furniture for all the people. Aside from Steve's she did not see one face she knew. Her mood, already crazed and a little concerned, dipped into the despairing range.

"There they are, Bren, two hundred fifty of our closest friends," Brandon shouted over the noise.

It wasn't her fault the guest list had gotten out of hand. Obviously, she hadn't made it clear enough that the guests she invited should be careful who *they* invited. But they should have known when she said A list, that's what she meant.

None of that mattered now. Desperate times called for desperate measures. "We'll throw some of them out," Brenda said, and knew as she said it that weeding the crowd would be impossible.

Brandon shook his head. "Be my guest. Tell me where to begin and I'll even help you."

Sometime later—Brenda was not certain exactly how long it had been—she had picked up thousands of paper cups, tried to keep hundreds of people from grinding chips and dip into the carpet with their shoes, and had turned down the stereo at least three times. She had been doing this all her life and no end was in sight. In what circle of hell did the party-throwers reside?

Brenda ordered herself to get a grip. This was *her* house, and she was allowed to exercise a certain amount of control. It was in that frame of mind that she approached Kelly. Steve had just refilled her paper cup with something green and slushy. The famous triple M.

As Steve moved off, shaker held high, Brenda accosted Kelly by saying, "Can I talk to you for a second?"

"Okay. Okay. I did ask a few people from Beverly High, but—"

"That's all right. What's a few hungry faces more or less? I thought you weren't going to drink anymore."

"My mom drinks. I sip." By the way Kelly changed the subject, Brenda could tell she'd hit a nerve. Good. "What about you?" Kelly asked.

"I'm drinking cola when I have time."

"When you have time?"

"Have you any idea what a mess three hundred people can make? Neither Brandon nor I are drinking alcohol. We made a pact."

"I guess you didn't sign it in blood." Kelly nodded toward the foot of the stairway to the second floor.

Standing there with Steve, and of all people,

Drew, was Brandon. They were laughing and patting each other on the back and downing Steve's concoction as if there were no tomorrow.

All the anger that Brenda felt about the bloated party was suddenly concentrated on Brandon. She was on her way to let him know how she felt when yet another person came in the front door. "Am I in the right house?"

Thank goodness, it was Dylan. "I'm starting to wonder about that myself," Brenda said. She nearly fell into his arms with relief. Dylan had been around. He'd know what to do about everything.

Glass shattered in the kitchen.

"Oh my God," Brenda said, and ran toward the noise.

The retreat was being held at an old resort at the top of a winding road in the Santa Barbara Mountains, a shining white stucco building with the traditional red tile roof. The grounds were enormous and lush. The quiet somehow seemed to be part of the building.

Mr. and Mrs. Walsh had a beautiful room with all the amenities. They were just putting out the "Do Not Disturb" sign and starting to get cozy when a loud, grating, yet female voice cried, "How y'all doin'?" from a point inside their room.

Cindy and Jim Walsh sprang apart, somehow guilty despite their age and the fact that they were married, and found two strangers standing in front of the door between their room and the next room over.

The woman wore a pant suit in a shade of electric blue not often seen outside a new car showroom. Blond hair was piled in an improbable tower on top of her head. She smiled broadly, allowing her back teeth to show. The man next to her wore a dark suit that had Wild West piping around the pockets. His smile barely showed any teeth at all and his hands moved nervously at his side. His gray hair was combed over to hide his bald spot. They both wore elaborate cowboy boots.

As she crossed the room with her hand extended the woman cried, "Didn't mean to interrupt anything. We're your neighbors." She seemed never to speak below an enthusiastic bellow. "I'm Trudy Barnett," she said as she pumped Jim's hand. "And this is my husband, Bob. From the Houston office? Say howdy, Bob."

Bob made a small nod in their direction.

"He's the shy type till he gets to know you," Trudy said.

"Trudy," said Bob in a normal voice, "I think they want some privacy."

"Oh, pooh. The point of these retreats is

meeting new people and sharing ideas." She looked Jim square in the eyes and asked, "Isn't that right, darlin'?"

Both Jim and Cindy were overwhelmed and therefore momentarily speechless. Trudy didn't seem to notice. She asked, "So, where y'all from, anyway?"

Trudy and Bob quickly became their constant companions. Bob was really kind of sweet, and very much awash in Trudy's bad case of personality. During one of their rare moments of solitude, the Walshes asked the management to fix the lock on the door between their room and the Barnetts'. The management assured them it would be done immediately. Hoping to put the kiss of death on the relationship, Jim had mournfully assured Trudy that their table for the big banquet that evening was full, and Cindy had quickly backed him up.

While they dressed for the banquet that evening Jim and Cindy were congratulating themselves on how well they had handled things when a familiar voice called, "Knock, knock!"

Apparently, the management had not fixed the lock well enough to discourage Trudy and Bob. Trudy stood just inside the Walsh room bearing champagne and four glasses. Peeking out from behind her, Bob smiled meekly and held a plate of cheese and crackers. Trudy ignored or did not notice the reticence with which Cindy invited them in.

As she poured, Trudy said, "Dom Perignon eighty-five. Just a little treat to show how much we enjoyed your company this afternoon. Right, Bob?"

Bob smiled and set down his plate.

"And it turns out we have a little celebrating to do too. I talked to that maître d' fellow and it turns out there's *plenty* of room at your table this evening. Isn't that great?"

The banquet was a long formal affair, and Trudy kept up a running commentary on what they ate, what people around them wore, and the relative merits of the speakers. At one point she said, "You two are so sweet. Bob and I were talking about visiting y'all in Beverly Hills. Wouldn't that be a gas?"

Neither of the Walshes knew what to say to that, but filling a silence was never a problem for Trudy.

The dancing started and the Walshes watched for their chance to escape. It finally came when Trudy was distracted by her own efforts to whip everyone into a cowboy frenzy singing "The Yellow Rose of Texas."

"I can't hear you!" Trudy cried as she sang and made big conducting motions.

With Trudy's attention elsewhere, Jim

grabbed Cindy's hand and they slipped out to return to their room. They were ready for a little entertainment of a more private nature. Jim was kissing behind Cindy's right ear when she leaped away from him and said, "I have to do one thing first." Ignoring her husband's pained expression, she called home.

"Party line."

"Brenda?"

"No, er, hi, Mrs. Walsh. This is Kelly. Just a minute, I'll get her for you." The phone was muffled for a few seconds, then Brenda came on the line sounding chipper.

"Hi, Mom. How's Santa Barbara?"

"We're having a wonderful time. What's all that noise?"

"Donna and Kelly are here." Brenda shouted to someone at her end. "Donna, turn down the stereo!"

"Let me say hello to Brandon."

"Mom, Brandon's upstairs and the pizza man just arrived. Got to go. Love you and Daddy."

"Love you, too. See you Sunday."

Impatient, Jim grabbed his wife from behind and began to nuzzle. "Everything all right at home?"

"Sounds like it."

■ ■ ■

As Brenda hung up the phone, Donna timidly gave her the bad news. Brenda was horrified. She wanted to find Dylan, but that probably wouldn't sit well with Brandon. As the man of the house, Brandon would feel he had to take care of this latest development.

But Brandon was still drinking with Steve and Drew. As upset as Brenda was, she pulled the paper cup from Brandon's hand and said, "I thought we had a pact?"

Brandon's movements were a little sloppy and standing up seemed to be a feat of which he was barely capable. He said, "First you holler because I'm too responsible. Now you have a problem because I'm too loose. What gives?"

"What gives, Brandon, is that a police car is parked in front of this house. I don't think they're here to pick up girls."

"I'll take care of it," Brandon said cockily, and walked stiffly toward the door.

8

Plan B

THE POLICE WON'T BE A PROBLEM,
Brandon thought. It's our house, after all.
We're just having a party. It was a free country,
wasn't it?

There came a polite knocking at the door.

Brandon drew himself up and said, "I'll do
the talking."

Dylan came up next to him and said, "Do
anything you want, bro, but if those cops catch
a whiff of your breath, they'll bust you for
sure."

The knocking became louder and more
insistent.

"Okay," Brandon said. He knew Dylan was right, but that didn't make it any easier to give up being the responsible one. "Just don't let them in."

Brandon retreated to the foot of the stairway and sat down a little harder than he'd intended. He looked around for his cup and couldn't find it. By this time Brenda had opened the front door and was standing there next to Dylan. Facing them were a pair of cops—one old enough to be their father, and the other more like college age.

Brightly, Brenda said, "Hi, officers. Is there a problem?"

The old cop said, "Is this your house?" He sounded like a no-nonsense type, maybe with kids of his own whom he kept on a very short leash.

"Yes, sir," Brenda said. Brandon appreciated how good she was at sounding polite.

"Are your parents home?"

"Not at the moment. But they'll be back soon."

"Yeah," the old cop said. "Like about Sunday night."

The young cop smiled and asked, "Did it occur to you that most of your neighbors would probably not care to hear 'Jamajamarama' at this hour?"

We're in deep now, Brandon thought.

Jason Priestley as Brandon Walsh.

Gabrielle Carteris and Jason Priestley as Andrea Zuckerman and Brandon Walsh.

Brian Austin Green as David Silver.

Shannen Doherty as Brenda Walsh.

"Stop, before you break my heart." Kelly, Brenda, and Donna perform. *From the left:* Jennie Garth, Shannen Doherty, and Tori Spelling.

"T.V.'s most on-and-off again couple." Jennie Garth and Ian Ziering.

Luke Perry as Dylan McKay.

A light moment on the set with Jason Priestley and Gabrielle Carteris.

Tori Spelling as Donna Martin.

Luke Perry and Jason Priestley.

The kids of West Beverly High. From left to right: Ian Ziering, Jennie Garth, Tori Spelling, Brian Austin Green, Gabrielle Carteris, Jason Priestley, Shannen Doherty, and Luke Perry.

Maybe I should have handled it after all.

Dylan said to Brenda, "I'm sorry. You were right. My cousin begged me not to pump up the volume, but see, it's her birthday, and—"

"It's your birthday?" the young cop asked excitedly. "My birthday was last Wednesday."

Brandon realized that the young cop was kind of a geek. But that could only work in their favor.

"Hey, happy birthday," Brenda said.

Meanwhile, the old cop became more and more unhappy. He tried to get a look inside the house without leaving the front step. This was Beverly Hills, after all. Not even the police entered a house uninvited. Who knew who these kids had for parents? "How many kids do you have in there?"

Hundreds, Brandon thought. Thousands.

Before either Brenda or Dylan needed to answer, the young cop managed to convince his partner that they could be off catching criminals rather than badgering kids who were having a good time in their own home.

Grousing, the old cop said, "Just keep the damned music down, understand?"

Brandon didn't notice quite how it happened, but the next thing he knew, the police were gone. Brandon admired the way Dylan and Brenda had handled them. Just the way he would have done if they'd let him. Steve wrapped Brandon's fingers around a full cup of mucho marvelous margarita.

"Maybe I shouldn't," Brandon said. He was a little shaky, and he knew it.

"Of course you should," Steve said. "This stuff is full of vitamin T."

"T?"

"For tequila."

They both laughed, and Brandon drank up. When he lowered his cup, Dylan was standing there with a disapproving expression on his face. He offered to make Brandon a cup of coffee, but had barely gotten started on his temperance lecture when Brandon saw Andrea arrive.

"Excuse me," Brandon said. "I must greet my guest."

Andrea looked around, amused, and said sarcastically, "A few of your friends?"

"We be really stylin', no?"

Andrea told Brandon about the great play she'd just seen. He nodded and smiled, but the truth was, he couldn't quite catch her drift. Complicated play, he thought. Worse than Shakespeare.

"Wanta dance?" Brandon asked. He pulled her to him and they shuffled around a little. This is great, Brandon thought while he held Andrea close. She could be a real fox if she would just loosen up a little. Kelly Taylor danced by with some freshman who wasn't even supposed to be there. He wondered what could possibly be going on till he saw Steve watching them with murder in his eyes. Steve-avoidance was going on, and the geek was the beneficiary.

Yes, Andrea could be a really cute girl if she didn't always dress like a teacher. He gave her a big smooch right on the mouth. Her mouth was hot and wet and soft, and she kissed back for a moment. Suddenly she pulled away and caught her breath while she stared at him, astonished.

"Brandon, you're drunk," she said.

"So?" What else was new? Brandon wondered.

"So, I've never seen you drunk before, and the first time I do, you kiss me."

This was incredible. First Brenda, then Dylan, now Andrea. Angrily, he said, "I finally get to a place where I can let myself kick back, and hey, it turns out that nobody but me can handle it."

"Maybe that's because you're *not* handling it. I'll see you Monday. Take care of yourself."

With some surprise Brandon watched her march right out of there. She couldn't get away with this. It was his party and he could get drunk if he wanted to. And if he wanted to do a little slow dancing with the editor of the school paper, that should be all right, too.

He was about to go after her when Steve grabbed him by the arm and said, "Meltdown, bro. The liquor is no longer."

"Major bummer."

"Can we get into your parents' private stash?"

"Don't even *think* about it."

"Then we need to put into effect Plan B."

"Plan B?"

Brenda and Dylan were in the backyard sitting side by side on a picnic bench, looking deep into the shadows. The night was beautiful, and Brenda was relieved to be away from the madhouse behind them. The party could have been in another world. As a matter of fact, that would have been preferable. But it was too real. Sitting here with Dylan was comfortable. He was laid-back, and not even remotely drunk.

Still, it was her party, and the confrontation with the police had unnerved her. The music was no softer than it had been and it wasn't getting any earlier. If the police came back and shut the party down, her parents would certainly hear about it. Brenda could not allow that to happen. Brandon was obviously in no condition to be the responsible one. It was all up to her, and she was not entirely comfortable with the job.

As if she had made a final decision, she

said, "I'll give it till twelve-thirty. Then I pull the plug."

"All right," Dylan said. He was smoothing her hair so that it hooked behind her ear. Very nice.

Brenda continued to agonize. Twelve-thirty was actually kind of early. "Maybe one o'clock. But that's the absolute latest."

"Right," said Dylan, and nodded.

"What if they won't leave?"

"Then we'll have a slumber party."

She punched him in the shoulder.

"Don't worry. I'll help you throw the bums out. For a small nominal fee."

She leaned close to him. She knew what the fee would be, but she asked anyway.

"Oh, the usual," he said.

He leaned toward her. They kissed, and Brenda felt the heavenly jolt she always felt when she kissed Dylan. Out front, a car started, and she was yanked out of her romantic mood. Fearing the worst, she ran down the driveway and was just in time to see Steve tearing off in one direction in his Corvette, and Brandon tearing off in the other in Mondale.

Dylan placed a firm hand on her shoulder.

Brenda said, "Neither one of them should be driving."

"Sometimes God protects fools."

"Yeah, right."

"Worrying won't do any good. And some-times you just have to let a guy be a jerk. That's the only way he'll find out he *shouldn't* be a jerk."

"You're right." But Brenda was still wor-ried. She turned around, put her head on Dylan's shoulder, and said, "Let's dance."

Cindy and Jim Walsh were so keyed up they couldn't get comfortable in the room. They decided that a nice laze in the hot tub would be just what they needed. Because the hour was very late, their project seemed that much more exotic and erotic. They never could have done this at home.

They quietly followed a flagstone path to where the hot tub was hidden among hibiscus bushes, banana trees, and dwarf palms. It was empty. They sighed as they lowered them-selves into the creaming water, and then leaned against each other, allowing the hot turbulence to suck away their aches, their pains, and their thoughts of Trudy and Bob.

"I hear high heels on flagstones," Cindy whispered to her husband.

They decided that with their luck, the heels had to belong to Trudy. But before they could escape, Trudy and Bob, wearing matching ter-rycloth robes, appeared from behind a hedge.

Trudy said, "We've been looking all over for

you lovebirds to see if you'd take a little splish-splash with us, and here you are."

"Actually, we were just getting out," Jim said. He and Cindy reached for their own robes as they rose.

"Now, don't be an old party poop, Jim Walsh. The fun's just starting."

"How are you tonight, Cindy?" Bob asked.

Cindy looked at her husband for guidance, found none, and said, "Just fine, Bob. How are you?"

"I'm game," Bob said.

Jim nodded as if Bob had said something smart. Suddenly Jim turned to his wife. "Speaking of games, you know, dear, we have that tennis game early tomorrow. Very early tomorrow."

"Oh, come on, Jimbo," Trudy said. "What has a little ol' tennis game got to offer that I don't?" Trudy threw off her robe. She stood there in the landscaping light, a white overblown goddess, somewhat past middle age and not wearing a stitch. With somewhat less flair Bob also let his robe fall. He stood next to Trudy smiling shyly, but looking surprisingly muscular.

"We have to go now," Cindy said stiffly. She and Jim carefully backed through the hedge where there had not been a path before. By the time they got back to their room they were both laughing nervously. They went to bed and lay next to each other woodenly, as if in shock. Every so often one of them would say wonderingly, "They seemed so normal," and the other would nod.

The telephone rang and they looked at it as if it were a poisonous animal in striking distance.

"It's two in the morning," Jim said angrily. "If that's them, I'm going to the management committee."

The phone rang again, and Cindy picked up the receiver, a worried expression on her face.

9

The bright side

"HELLO?"

Brenda felt comforted just hearing her mom's voice. "Hello, Mom? It's me, Brenda."

"Hi, Brenda. What's wrong?" Cindy's voice was tense.

Just like Mom. She could tell more from the tone of her voice than other people could tell by peeking into her diary. The fact was that Brenda was emotionally drained. She had already done all her crying, mostly onto poor Dylan's shoulder. She was still upset, but her overloaded body could do nothing more about it. She was limp. Calling from a phone in the lobby of the police station did not improve her mood.

Brenda took a deep ragged breath and quickly told her mom what had happened. Not even admitting that she'd been arrested for shoplifting had been so difficult. She said, "Brandon was in a car accident tonight."

"What?"

"But he's okay." She heard her mom repeat the news to her dad. She knew what was coming next. The ritual handing-off of the telephone, the sharing of the receiver.

"Brenda, what happened?" Dad asked anxiously.

"Brandon was driving alone, so I don't really know, but he's okay."

"Was anyone else hurt?"

"No. Nobody was in the other car, but Mondale got totaled." Brenda felt herself slipping. Evidently, more tears were left in her, and she shed them now. "When I saw the car, I was sure he was dead." Her voice caught in her throat.

"Where is Brandon now, honey?"

What could Brenda say? As long as Brandon was all right, what did it matter where he was? But it *did* matter to her, and she knew it would matter to her parents.

"Brenda?"

Finally she blurted it out. "He's in jail,

Daddy. They arrested him for drunk driving."

There was heavy breathing at the other end of the phone. Dylan had not known how to ease her pain, and she had no idea how to ease the pain of her parents. She said the only thing she could think of at the moment. "I'm sorry, Daddy."

Jail was a really terrible place. Not just because of the bars and the metal walls and the smell of human failure and the sounds of human anger. Nothing on TV or in the movies could convey the overwhelming *cold* of the place. Oh, the air was warm enough; the cold was spiritual.

The worst part about being there was that Brandon knew he deserved it. He had done something mind-bogglingly stupid, and he was just beginning to pay for it. Even pushing the speed limit, his parents would need two hours to drive down from Santa Barbara. It would be four or even five o'clock before they got there. He didn't know how long he'd been in his cell already. He didn't think it was morning yet, but he felt as if he'd been in the can for years.

When the policeman came to get him, he didn't really care where he was going. He only wanted out.

Mom and Dad stood up when he was

brought into the dull utilitarian lobby. They looked as if they'd had a bad night, but he suspected he looked worse. He felt grubby in a way that soap would not cleanse. The policeman behind the desk had everybody sign papers and then lost interest. He had phones to answer.

Mom touched Brandon's arm and asked, "Are you okay?"

What? Physically? Spiritually? Emotionally? Brandon shrugged and said, "Yeah," because it's what he knew everybody wanted to hear.

"Yeah?" Mr. Walsh said. His voice was tinged with disbelief and anger.

Brandon didn't want to discuss anything. He just wanted to get out of there. They could itemize his sins later. He said, "Yeah. So how was the retreat?"

His father shook his head and said, "Brandon, come here," and opened his arms.

Brandon and his dad hugged. Dad was solid, sensible, a thing to hang on to in a world gone mad with Brandon's own madness. Brandon blinked away the tears of overwhelming relief. "I'm sorry, Dad," he said quietly.

"I know you are. We'll get through this somehow."

"They're going to take away my license, aren't they?"

"You can count on it."

Brandon shook his head at his own previous feelings of invulnerability. He stood away from his father and said, "That's the last time I ever throw a party."

"Party?" Mom asked. "What party?"

"Brenda and I sort of threw a party."

That was not a sufficient explanation, of course, but Brandon was a hollow man, and he didn't know what else to say. He suggested that Brenda could give them any answers they might need. They left him alone for the duration of the ride home, but even from the back-seat, Brandon could sense his parents' bottled-up frustration and curiosity.

When they got home, Brandon held his breath as Dad opened the front door. His parents stood in the foyer, stunned at the remains of the party. Paper cups and small cocktail plates were everywhere. Splats of dip and puddles of dark liquid dotted the carpet. Crumpled paper napkins were piled in drifts like snow. Lampshades were askew and, in at least one case, missing. Someone had pulled the cushions off the couch and made a fort of them in front of the fireplace. Brandon slunk in and slouched against the archway between the foyer and the living room.

Brenda stood motionless among the carnage holding a stack of dirty plates and cups and looking guilty as hell. She tried on a smile, but it died for lack of sincerity.

Trying very hard to be reasonable, Dad asked, "Would you care to explain what happened here, Brenda?"

"We invited a few friends over, and, well, I guess it got a little out of hand." There was that smile again. Brandon didn't think it would work, and it didn't.

"A little out of hand," their father exclaimed. "You and your friends trashed this place."

"My friends aren't the ones who did this."

"Is that better, Brenda? You let strangers into this house—strangers who drank and caroused and had no respect for your property?"

"A hundred fifty extra people all showed up at once. Some of the guys brought liquor. What were we supposed to do?"

"Lock the door."

Brandon wondered if Dad knew how ridiculous that suggestion sounded. Brandon wanted to help Brenda deal with their parents, but he had dealt with enough that evening.

Brenda revved herself up to a fit of righteousness. She said, "Look, Dad—"

"No, *you* look, Brenda. You look me in the eye and tell me how we're ever supposed to trust you kids again."

"That's not fair. *I* didn't drink."

"How do I know you're telling the truth?"

Still clutching the pile of trash, Brenda

turned away from him.

This had gone far enough. Drained as he was, Brandon couldn't stand the badgering anymore. Somebody had to defend Brenda, and he was elected. Without moving from his place against the wall, he spoke loudly. "She wasn't drinking, Dad. I was."

While still looking at Brenda, Dad said, "I know. I read the police report."

Brandon could think of nothing to say to that.

Brenda set down the trash and faced her parents again. Her cheeks were flushed with anger. "You don't know how much pressure there is on guys to drink these days, Dad."

Wrong, Bren, wrong. Brandon didn't want to be made out as some fashion dweeb—somebody who followed the crowd so he could be part of it. He said. "That's not what happened. I can't explain it."

Mom said, "Well, you have to try, Brandon. Ever since you threw up at Foster's Lake, you made a big deal about how stupid drinking was."

"And it still is. But last night some jerk handed me a cup of punch. By the time I found out it was spiked, I was half-petrified." That was not exactly what had happened the night before, but it was kind of what had happened at Donna's. It's what had triggered this whole drinking episode. He shook his head. "I guess you could say I screwed up. I guess you could say I'm not perfect."

His admission seemed to satisfy his parents for the moment. Dad promised to call a lawyer Monday morning. Brenda's expression was unreadable. She had not done time, but she also had not had an easy evening.

Everybody slept late the next morning. Lying there in bed, Brandon decided that he'd felt better, but he didn't feel as bad as he had the night before. At least the large hollow place inside was gone. And he gave himself good advice about getting used to life without Mondale. The wonderful smells rising from the kitchen encouraged him to get up.

Mom made a real Sunday breakfast with pancakes and eggs and sausages and juice and coffee. Conversation was sparse till Dad made a stab at healing his family's wounds by saying lightly, "Well, coming back a day early really wasn't so bad. At least we got away from Trudy and Bob."

"Trudy and Bob?" Brandon asked. He didn't really care, but if Dad was going to make a gesture, the least he could do was cooperate. He'd gotten off very easy. So far, anyway.

Brenda seemed very involved in her food. Brandon knew she didn't like being called a liar, and it would be a while before she forgot how angry she was and gave her father a break.

Mom and Dad had a good time telling the saga of Trudy and Bob, and by the time they were done everybody at the table was laughing. Even Brenda had cracked a smile.

Brandon spent most of the afternoon immersing himself in the oily technical details of repairing, revamping, and revitalizing his bicycle. For a long time it would be his only transportation to school and to the Peach Pit.

He was putting 3-In-One oil on the chain when Brenda came outside to glower at him.

"Why are you looking at me like that?" Brandon asked. "I stood up for you this time. I didn't let you take the fall."

"You also didn't tell the truth. Nobody spiked your drink, Brandon."

"They did at Donna's."

"Yeah. But after that nobody held a gun to your head forcing you to down Steve's brew all evening."

Brandon gaped at Brenda in disbelief. "You know, Brenda, I'm coming off the worst night of my life. And if I have to bend the chronology of my downfall a little to get through it, I was hoping that certain people would cut me a little slack."

Brenda didn't say anything to that. When she went back into the house, Brandon was glad. He didn't need that kind of noise at the moment. He turned his attention back to the bike.

At the hearing the following week, the lawyer Dad found pointed out that Brandon had no criminal record and that he'd never driven drunk before. The judge ruled that in three weeks Brandon could apply for permission to drive up and back to school and to work. Meanwhile, he was strictly limited to two wheels. With Mondale so much scrap iron, Brandon was certain that he'd be using his bicycle for a lot longer than the law required. Heck, he deserved it.

That evening, Dylan strolled into the Peach Pit at about closing. Nat insisted on serving him a huge order of peach pie à la mode and coffee. Brandon was filling saltshakers and napkin holders when Dylan said quietly, "Kelly is spreading the word that the party at your house was the best so far this season."

"Mom and Dad will be so pleased," Brandon said.

"Don't be bitter, man. You got off lucky."

"Yeah. Just another learning experience. All Brenda and I have to do is pay the cleaning bills and replace all the broken stuff."

"And nobody got killed."

"The bright side, right?" Brandon had heard all this before and he was tired of it. If this entire situation had a bright side, it was that he had concrete evidence what a doofus he could be.

That kind of knowledge was useful for preventing a guy from getting a swelled head. "What about the dark side? Mom and Dad have been cool, but there's a big cloud over our house with a flashing neon sign inside that says DISAPPOINTMENT."

Dylan smiled sympathetically but did not speak.

"But that's nothing compared to the memory of when I hit the other car. I thought I was going to die. I can't get that sound out of my head." He began to energetically wipe down the counter, pretending he was wiping out the memory. "And even worse than that is pretending that I'm okay so that everybody else will be happy. I'm not okay, and I don't know how to deal with it."

Dylan nodded. "All you want to do is escape, right?"

"Yeah, but I don't know where to go. I lost my compass."

"I know just the place." Brandon looked at him questioningly, but Dylan seemed suddenly mesmerized by his coffee. With a quick push, he jumped off his stool and grabbed the rag out of Brandon's hand.

Dylan helped Brandon and Nat close the Peach Pit, and then he took Brandon for a little ride to a place he knew well.

10

Not a slumber party

BRANDON DIDN'T GET IT. DYLAN DROVE him to West Beverly High. At night it was a creepy place, half-lost in shadow like a haunted Victorian mansion. Dylan refused to give any explanation, but he seemed to have a particular destination in mind.

Silently, they walked along the wide empty halls to an open classroom where the lights were on. A small group of students was sitting around a middle-aged woman who had the air of a favorite teacher or a trusted parent.

Brandon soon realized, much to his surprise, that this was a meeting of Alcoholics

Anonymous. All these kids had drinking problems. Brandon was shocked by what happened next.

"Hi there. I'm Dylan. I'm an alcoholic."

The rest of the meeting was a kaleidoscope of personal stories, both horrifying and hilarious, occasionally both at once. Gallons of coffee were consumed. Brandon liked the way the members supported each other. They had all been through the same terrible places, and now they were helping each other stay out.

After the meeting, as Dylan drove Brandon home, Brandon said, "I guess I'm not the only one with a problem."

"You're definitely not alone."

Knowing he was not alone was a comfort, and Brandon thought it would help him put the terrible experience behind him, help him get on with his life. Still, those kids at the meeting couldn't watch him twenty-four hours a day. He was the only one who could do that. The weight of responsibility settled on his shoulders.

Inside the house, Brandon found his dad on the couch pretending to read the same novel his mom used for such purposes. They were both nervous. Neither of them knew where to begin. Brandon decided to begin at the beginning, with the lie that Brenda had already nailed him on.

"The other night at the famous party wasn't

the first time I had a drink," he said.

Dad nodded. He appeared neither surprised nor angry. He said, "I figured as much."

"How did you know?" Brenda would never tell. She could be a flake, but she was also stubbornly loyal.

"Believe it or not, I was your age once."

"And you lived to tell about it?"

Dad nodded again. "You make choices, Brandon. That's what life's all about."

The AA people had said the same thing. Maybe it was true. Not always easy, but always true.

Brandon felt very warm toward his dad at the moment. The guy could be an old bear, but when he calmed down, he could be understanding and give useful advice. Not always easy, but always useful. They sat together in comfortable silence until Brandon said he was heading upstairs.

Brandon had a lot to think over while he got ready for bed. When he climbed into the sack at last, he picked up a photograph that had been lying nearby. It showed him and Mondale in happier times. The dear departed. Brandon was really lucky nobody had been killed. Nobody but poor Mondale, his first car, his prize. He felt as if he'd lost a pet.

Brenda, dressed in a long flannel nightgown, knocked on his doorjamb. She sat down on Brandon's bed and studied the photo over his shoulder. "I was thinking," she said, "about how I felt when I saw the wreck, as if I'd lost you forever."

"Brenda, I'm fine."

"I know." Brenda seemed to have difficulty speaking her mind. "I was just thinking that life is so unpredictable anyway, that it's really stupid to do *anything* that you know for a fact is dangerous."

"You came in here to tell me I'm stupid?"

"No, dummy. I came in here to tell you I love you." She kissed him, leaving one of her tears on his cheek, and then ran from the room.

Brandon was sorry that he'd dragged his family through Hell, but the glow left behind when they all discovered how much they loved each other almost made the whole thing worthwhile. Almost.

The following week, Brenda read a magazine article about the importance of female bonding, and she conceived the idea of a night gathering without boys. The event would *not* be a slumber party, despite the persistence of that misunderstanding by Brandon, her parents, and even her friends.

But the slumber-party misunderstanding was not Brenda's most difficult problem. The whole drunken-orgy question had not yet blown over, and Brenda thought it unlikely that her parents would allow another teen party in their house before the next ice age.

But Brenda lobbied hard. She made many promises—among them the acceptance of her mom as chaperon, and that the guest list would be limited and subject to parental approval. The promises would limit her independence, but they would also improve her chances that the bonding would happen at all.

At last her parents agreed, as kind of a test of Brenda's responsibility. Dad would stay upstairs. Mom would chaperon. And Brandon, she prayed, would find something to do away from the house.

When Brenda announced her success to Kelly and Donna, their reaction was less enthusiastic than she might have wished.

"Are you sure this thing is not a slumber party?" Kelly asked as they strolled through the crowded halls to class. "I mean, we gave up that sort of thing in junior high."

Brenda sighed. "Why is this so difficult for everyone to understand? It's an evening of female bonding, a chance for us to talk about what's important to us as women."

"But we're doing it in our nightgowns," Donna said.

"Unless you would prefer to sleep in your

clothes," Brenda said, not sparing the sarcasm.

"Why don't we invite some guys over for later?" Kelly said. "I mean after we've talked and bonded and everything."

"Kelly," Brenda said with extreme patience, "we want to have a single night out of our entire lives when we don't have to *think* about guys, don't have to *talk* about guys, don't have to *worry* about what we look like because some guys are around."

"Actually, that's not the problem. I sort of made plans with this other friend of mine, Amanda Peyser. You don't know her, but we've been friends forever."

"Bring her along."

"I would," Kelly said, "except that I don't want her to think it's a slumber party. It isn't a slumber party, right?"

Before Brenda had a chance to answer, they rounded a corner and came face-to-face with Steve Sanders and Brandon. Steve put on his trademark smirk and said, "'Morning, girls. Got your nighties all ready for this evening?"

This was really too much. Steve was a total jerk. Kelly said, "Sorry you have to miss it, Steve. I hear that cheap thrills are about all you're getting these days."

Steve goggled at her, speechless.

Wow, Brenda thought. Where does she get it?

Brenda and Kelly walked on, heads held

high. Behind her, Brenda heard Donna say, "Left you in the dust, son."

That evening, Brenda was already in her nightgown by eight. It was, as she explained to Brandon, a tradition.

"Maybe in Minnesota. Here in Bev Hills it's just weird."

Brenda studied the inside of the refrigerator and wondered if a single case of diet soda would be enough. Rather than engaging Brandon in a discussion for which she was in no mood, she asked, "Aren't you and Steve supposed to be going out tonight to do manly-man stuff?"

"He'll be by. How come Dad gets to stay here?"

From the kitchen table, where he and Mom were finishing dinner, her dad said, "Because it's my house."

Mom said, "And because you promised to stay upstairs."

Brandon shook his head and smiled. "Right," he said. "No guys allowed. But you and I both know that guys will be the main topic of conversation."

Brenda decided that her brother was having too much fun at her expense. "This may come as a shock to you, Brandon," she said, "but we have many other, much more important things on our minds."

Brandon snapped his fingers. "That's right.

I forgot Andrea is coming." To their parents he went on, "She told me she was going to some kind of women's conference tonight. But I nailed her when she admitted it was happening here. You're right, Bren. Andrea will probably engage you in a meaningful discussion about socioeconomic problems in third-world nations."

For a moment, Brenda feared that Brandon was correct. But she did not have long to fret because the doorbell rang. Brandon ran for it, and then called from the foyer, "Brenda, Kelly and Donna are here to bond with you."

After that, Brandon left with Steve, Dad went upstairs, and only women were left below. Brenda's guests looked a little embarrassed to be there. Kelly explained that Amanda might be along later. "This is probably a little down-home for her."

"It's not a hayride," Brenda said. "You guys go upstairs and change. Dad's camping out in the bedroom. He has no excuse to emerge. He has a TV, a bowl of popcorn, an entire library of paperback science fiction, and a bathroom."

As she and Donna ascended, Kelly said, "All right, but I'm warning you: I don't have a nightgown. I wear a man's silk pajamas."

"Which man?" Brenda asked. Her mom and Donna laughed.

We will not talk about guys, Brenda

promised herself. We will *not*.

When Kelly came down wearing her silk pajamas, she looked like a vamp in some old movie. Donna wore a flannel nightgown similar to Brenda's. Andrea apparently slept in something very much like a jogging outfit.

The bonding took a while to get off the ground. They lit a fire in the fireplace, but it kept going out. Kelly, whose mom had a cabin at Arrowhead, reset the logs and threw in some old newspaper, and got it running at last. The fire roared and crackled and heat poured out at them. They talked about other times, other places, other fires, but soon the talk died and they just stared morosely into the flames.

Brenda was afraid that the whole evening would be a bust. But then she put on some wild dance music, and they formed a conga line that snaked around the living room. For a moment no one seemed to care whether this was a slumber party or not.

They were really getting into it when Mom came in with guacamole and chips. Brenda and her friends insisted that anyone who entered the room *must* dance. At first Mom resisted the invitation, but then she outdanced them all with some weird moves from the sixties.

While Mom was showing them how to do the watusi the doorbell rang, and she made her escape. She let in a tall gaunt girl wearing a dressy suit that might have been very hip around some corporate office, but seemed kind of like overkill for a Saturday-night bonding.

Brenda knew that making snap judgments about people was unfair and generally wrong, but something about this girl was nasty. For one thing she stood at the edge of the foyer as if just looking at the crowd in the living room was beneath her and a little painful.

Kelly, appearing to be a little uncomfortable herself, introduced Amanda Peyser, the person who had been her friend, like forever. Loudly enough for Brenda and the others to hear, Amanda whispered to Kelly from the side of her mouth, "I thought you said this *wasn't* a slumber party."

Trying to be gracious, especially because her mother was watching, Brenda said, "Amanda, if you want a nightgown or something, I have plenty of extras."

Amanda smiled at Brenda without sincerity and asked if she could speak to Kelly alone.

When they had both left the room, Donna said, "Amanda seems a little stuck-up."

"Yeah," said Andrea. "If her nose was any higher, she could balance a ball on the end of it."

They all laughed at that and barked like seals, but the truth was, Amanda didn't seem to be very interested in making friends. As the night wore on, she always stood off to one side,

kind of observing them as if they were a herd
of bizarre animals. And somewhere, she had
learned the Steve Sanders smirk.

When they all trooped into the kitchen to
raid the refrigerator, Brenda took that opportunity to ask Kelly what the story was on
Amanda.

"She tried to get me to go to some frat
party with her, but I told her that I was staying
here."

"Thanks, Kel."

"No biggie. I've been to frat parties. I'm
having a better time here than I've had at most
of them."

"Why is *she* hanging around?"

Kelly glanced into the kitchen. "I don't
think she wants to go alone, and I don't blame
her. Some of those guys seem to have eight
hands. She's waiting for me to get bored."

"Are you bored?" Brenda asked worriedly.

"Not unless you're out of chocolate chip,"
Kelly said, and smiled.

There was bright jovial chaos in the kitchen
as everybody scooped their favorite ice cream
into big bowls and then added toppings that surprised Brenda, some because she had been certain that she was the only one with a particular
perversion, and some because a perversion was
one she'd never even considered. For instance
it turned out that Donna liked popcorn with her

ice cream. Everyone but Donna (and Amanda,
who had no opinion) thought this was gross.

Brenda turned to Amanda—who was
watching from the doorway—and asked,
"Would you like some ice cream?"

"Nothing for me, thanks."

Kelly looked critically at a tower of whipped
cream she had just spurted upon an edifice of
chocolate-chip ice cream, chocolate sauce, and
smushed peanut-butter cookies. She said,
"Come on, Amanda. You'll make us all feel like
cows."

"You said it," said Amanda. "I didn't."

Everyone stopped talking and laughing.
For the first time, Brenda realized that she had
about a zillion calories in her bowl. If eating
this stuff didn't taste so good, she might as well
apply it directly to her hips. But she couldn't
allow Amanda to ruin the bonding for everyone. Suddenly inspired, she bellowed, "Moo!"
right in Amanda's face.

They others laughed and began to moo.
They marched past the flabbergasted Amanda
with their ice cream, laughing and mooing.
When they were settled on the floor in the living room with their ice cream, Kelly said, "I
would never pig out like this when boys are
around."

Everyone agreed, which as far as Brenda
was concerned, made the ice cream all the

sweeter. She said, "I'm always too nervous to eat on a date."

Kelly said, "Plus, it ruins your makeup and you never know how you look while you're chewing."

They all nodded. Amanda was sitting by herself on a chair, watching them sternly. Maybe she was just shy, Brenda thought, though she didn't believe it herself. Still, it was Brenda's house and she had certain obligations. "Do you eat on dates, Amanda?" she asked.

After a moment of consideration Amanda said, "Never. But I always order something expensive." She acted as if even speaking to them was contaminating her in some way.

"Why order something you're not going to eat?" Andrea asked.

"To let them know I'm worth it," Amanda said.

That was a new way to think about dating, as kind of a war of nerves. A little awed, Andrea said, "Wow."

Kelly said, "I knew it was over between Steve and me when I started to chow down when we went out to dinner."

They talked about food for a while, and dating, which was not quite like talking about boys. When the ice cream was gone, the girls lay among the wreckage of bowls, spoons, soda cans, and half-empty bags of cookies and chips. Donna burped musically. They all tried burping. Kelly was of the opinion that recreational burping was really more of a guy thing, and they stopped.

During the silence that followed, the only noises were of labored breathing, of moaning about being too full to move, and of Amanda squirming in her chair. Brenda was afraid that her evening was dying. Maybe they really ought to let Andrea tell them about third-world countries. It had to be better than lying on the floor listening to your fat thicken. Brenda sat up suddenly and said, "So, what do you guys want to do now?"

Donna wanted to see *Pretty Woman* again, which did not excite much interest.

Brenda picked up empty ice-cream bowls and said, "Look, you guys, we're not going to rent a movie, not even *Dirty Dancing*."

That got a laugh, which was what Brenda had in mind.

She went on: "The point of getting together is to talk about the female experience."

"I feel all talked out," Kelly said.

"How 'bout something to eat?"

Everybody groaned and threw pillows at Brenda. Andrea picked up the rest of the bowls and followed her into the kitchen. When they got there, Andrea said, "I have an idea that never fails. If this doesn't start a conversation, nothing will." She pulled a flat box from her overnight bag. Brenda looked at it and smiled.

When they got back into the living room, Amanda and Kelly seemed to be in the midst of an argument, which Brenda chose to ignore. They stopped abruptly as Brenda and Andrea sat down.

"Look what Andrea brought," Brenda said.

"A Ouija board," Donna cried. "Those things are so cool."

Kelly opened the box and removed the contents, a playing board and an arrow-shaped plastic slider. The board had the numbers zero to nine on it, plus the alphabet. The word *yes* was in one corner, and the word *no* in the other. At the top was a picture of a creepy-looking woman wearing a turban. "What do you do with it?" Kelly asked.

"If the energy is right," Andrea said, "you can talk to those who have gone"—she paused dramatically— "beyond."

"Give me a break," Amanda said, and rolled her eyes.

Andrea said, "I wouldn't say that if I were you. This is a pretty powerful thing."

Nobody except Andrea knew any dead people, so they decided to contact her grandmother, who had a reputation for being really nice.

At Andrea's direction, Brenda turned off all

the electric lights in the living room. The girls sat around the board and put their fingertips on the Ouija slider. Even Amanda got involved, though she looked disgusted by the entire production.

"Now concentrate," Andrea said.

They waited for what seemed a long time. The ancient smell of burning wood somehow unhooked them from the present and from reality. The girls cast big dancing shadows in the firelight. Animals and other fiercely barbaric things lurked in the corners. The fire popped and they all jumped. They chuckled at their own fear, and Andrea got them to put their fingers on the slider again.

When the slider began to move, Brenda was certain that *she,* at any rate, was not pushing it. The other girls looked genuinely surprised, and even Amanda seemed impressed. The slider moved purposefully from letter to letter until it spelled out *I'm here.*

Andrea's jaw was tight and her eyes were wide. Maybe, Brenda thought, she wished she'd never started this. She looked into the air above the board and in a voice that shook only a little, said, "Gramma, is that you?"

A light flashed, and Andrea said, "She's here."

Brenda looked around. Her skin creeped.

"I'm scared," Donna said.

A light flashed again, and Kelly pointed to a window. They all screamed at the unnatural face staring in at them.

11

Manly-man stuff

BRANDON RODE NEXT TO STEVE IN THE very def black Corvette. All around them was the glitter, the glamour, the swank of Beverly Hills. It felt good just to be out and about in such a place—like maybe he was pretty swank himself.

Steve assured him that his black 'vette was catnip to girls. Brandon had a momentary flashback to his totaled car. Mondale had never been much on picking up girls—boiled carrots to Steve's catnip—but it had always gotten him home, which was, after all, what really counted.

Steve just drove around for a while, no destination in mind. He said, "We have to check out the sights. We don't want to favor just any establishment with our presence." A moment later he said, "You know, Brandon, your sister is really bold and bogus for throwing you out of your own house."

"I don't mind. Everybody, even Brenda, knows that what she has going is really a slumber party. She did me a big favor banishing me."

Steve hooted laughter. "Yeah, about now that party's probably crashing and burning. Girls need guys, Brandon. They can't have a good time without us."

If that was true, Brandon thought, it obviously worked the other way as well. What were he and Steve doing if not cruising for girls?

"There it is, Brandon, the garden of earthly delights." Steve pulled into the parking lot in front of a big black building that had fingers of light poking at the sky from the roof. Brandon should have guessed that Steve would take them to Floodlights. Word had been circulating for weeks that this was now the hottest place in existence.

"We can't get in there," Brandon said. "We're under age."

"Trust me, will you, Brandon? If all else fails, I'll slip the guy at the door a twenty or whatever it takes."

As they walked toward the big double doors Steve said hello to every unescorted female they passed. Brandon didn't know where these girls shopped, but it wasn't a hardware store. Steve got many smiles, a few titters, but no hits.

"You sure you can pick up a girl here, Steve?"

"If I can't, I can't pick one up anywhere."

"What happens when she wants to know where you work, where you live?"

"I'll tell her I work for my dad's import-export company and go to SC part-time. What do you do?"

Steve was outrageous. It was all so crazy it just might work. Why be normal? Brandon said, "I play professional hockey for the Kings."

"Get real, Brandon. Just say—" Steve took a moment with his hands over his eyes like a swami. "Just say you're taking a year off from UCLA to find yourself."

"Is that as good as being in your dad's import-export biz?"

"Trust me, Brandon. They'll eat it up with big spoons."

Brandon trusted Steve, but evidently the doorman did not. Not even Steve's ID, the twenty-dollar bill, could gain them entrance. And the thing that really rankled Steve was that the doorman pleasantly smiled through the entire rumpus.

Steve shoved the twenty back into his pocket, told the doorman, "This is the last time I ever come near this pigsty," and strode away as if he had big things to do somewhere else. "I can't believe this," he said to Brandon. "I think that geek actually enjoyed keeping us out."

They got into the car and Steve beat on the steering wheel. "I hate being underage," he cried.

"Steve."

"What?"

"If you brought your clever plastic Patrick Swayze disguise, now's the time to wear it."

"Huh?"

"Two of the hottest girls I've ever seen are coming this way."

Steve pumped a fist and whispered, "Yes!"

The two girls were straight out of a music video. One of them wore a miniskirt the size of a postage stamp and a Madonna sort of bustier that in an earlier life had perhaps been a bra. Her shiny black boots came up to her knees. The other one wore very short shorts and a shirt tied in the front. She wore red pumps with some of the sharpest heels Brandon had ever seen. Very hot, exciting girls.

The girl in the bra thing and the miniskirt leaned in at Brandon's side of the car. The girl in the pumps and short shorts leaned in at Steve. They introduced each other all around. The girl twirling Brandon's hair was Shelly. The one running her hands across the body of Steve's car as if it were alive was Trina.

Brandon could not tell which of them was better looking, but it was only the difference between terrific and incredible. Who would have thought girls like this would go for him and Steve? Brandon couldn't remember being so excited.

"It was so dead in there tonight," Shelly complained. "I don't blame you guys for bailing."

"Yeah," said Steve offhandedly, "this place is pretty beat."

"I love your car," Trina moaned. "It's so hot."

"It's transportation," Steve said, and shrugged. "So what are you ladies doing tonight?"

Shelly shot Brandon a look up from under. Bedroom eyes they called it in the old movies. Coyly she asked, "What did you gentlemen have in mind?"

Brandon knew what Steve had in mind, and the truth was, Brandon felt a little wild and crazy himself. These girls seemed up for it, but he had misread girls before.

While Brandon was looking into Shelly's eyes and frantically trying to figure out how to organize his evening, Steve invited the girls to go for a drive. Not bad, Brandon thought. The next logical move.

Shelly sat in Brandon's lap and Trina sat almost sideways between the two guys, with her arm around Steve. Shelly apologized for squishing Brandon, and Brandon told her not to worry. He knew that he had never been so happily squished in his life. Shelly admired Brandon's hair ("perfect convertible hair," she called it) and Brandon admired hers back. The conversation was dumb, but they both seemed to enjoy it.

Trina seemed less preoccupied with Steve than with Steve's car. The stick shift was of particular interest, which Brandon thought was pretty Freudian. Steve said, "In a sports car, a stick is the only way to go. It puts you at one with the road and with the machine."

To Brandon, that sounded like the kind of thing he heard in commercials.

"Sounds kind of Zen," Trina said.

Steve agreed and offered to let Trina shift the gears. The shifting of gears excited Trina, which excited Steve. He kept shooting Brandon knowing winks. Evidently, Steve was right. This was one time Brandon had not misread a woman who came on to him.

The girls were reticent to take Steve and Brandon to their apartment, and of course Steve and Brandon had no apartment of their own. "Our apartment is being earthquake-proofed tonight," Steve said, which sounded lame to Brandon, but the girls seemed to buy it.

As if uncertain of their reaction, Trina said, "I have an idea. Right near here is a really secluded playground behind an abandoned elementary school. We could go there and sort of, you know, talk. Get to know each other better." She casually let her manicured hand fall onto Steve's leg.

Steve and Brandon hurriedly agreed this was a fine idea.

Wild and crazy, Brandon thought. His skin could barely contain his energy.

The abandoned elementary school was not far away and the gate was already open. Apparently, others had used this playground. It was covered in blacktop, and the only light came from Steve's headlights and from the nearby street, which was not very near at all. Brandon could not see the yard's edges. The lights of Steve's 'vette picked out ancient four-square courts as he circled and came to a stop. The silence of the night closed in on them.

The girls were very eager. Shelly writhed in Brandon's arms as they kissed. Her body was tight and toned. Maybe she was a dancer. This was incredible. This sort of thing must happen in Minnesota, but it had never happened to him. Next to them, Trina and Steve were hard at it, hindered only a little by the presence of the stick shift and the steering wheel.

Between the wet smacks of kisses, Trina whispered something.

"What?" Steve asked, seemingly a little dazed.

It turned out that Trina wanted to drive Steve's car and she wanted to do it right now. "Please," she said breathlessly. "It would make me crazy." She suggestively ran her hands over the stick shift.

It was difficult for Brandon to believe that Trina could get much crazier, but Trina's declaration worked for Steve. He ordered everybody out of the car. Even Shelly seemed a little miffed. While she and Brandon watched, Steve climbed across to the passenger seat and Trina sat behind the wheel. She grabbed the stick shift with her right hand.

"She really likes cars," Shelly said to

Brandon, "but she could never afford anything this posh."

"I understand completely," Brandon said. He wondered briefly how these girls would have fit in at Brenda's slumber party.

Once again Steve told Trina about the H pattern in which the shift moved to change the gears. "First, second, third, fourth." Trina ran through the drill. "All right. Start the engine."

Trina started the engine and playfully gunned it. Steve suggested she let out the clutch. She did, but much too fast, and the engine stopped abruptly.

"That's okay," said Steve. "Try again."

Trina tried it again, and this time managed to jerk around the yard in a big circle. Brandon said, "If a guy drove Steve's car like that, Steve would kill him."

Shelly was grinning. "That looks like fun," she said.

When Steve and Trina came around again, Shelly called out, "Trina, I want a ride."

"She wants a ride," Brandon said, enjoying Steve's discomfort.

"*I'll* give you a ride," Steve said.

"No," said Shelly. "I want Trina to drive."

"Boss," Trina cried. "What do you say, Steve?" She looked at Steve and breathed at him and it was really no contest.

"Sure," he said. "Why not? Just be careful." He got out of the car slowly and Shelly got in. "Remember what I said now. Let the clutch out nice and easy."

"Right," Trina said.

"Bye," Shelly said, and waved at them.

The Corvette's engine roared, and a moment later it was out the gate and squealing as it turned into the street. Brandon was shocked, and Steve observed this with a wide-eyed sick expression on his face. As the engine thunder faded in the distance, he turned to Brandon and asked, "What's going on?"

"I don't know." Brandon knew. He suspected that if Steve were honest with himself, he knew, too. The air, previously warm with romance, was suddenly cold.

"They're just fooling around," Steve said confidently. "They'll be back."

Brandon frowned. Not far away, a main street rocked and rolled. The sound of Steve's 'vette was part of that rumble now, just another voice in the choir. Brandon said, "Steve, I think we've been had."

Steve went nose to nose with Brandon and shouted angrily, "Shut up, Brandon! They'll be back. And we're going to wait right here till they roll in." He walked away a few feet, kicked a rock, and thrust his hands into his pockets while he grimly stood watch on the driveway.

Brandon put his hands into his pockets and settled down to watch Steve. He wondered how long down would take before Steve admitted he would never see his car again.

12

Skeletons in the closet

WHEN THE LIGHT FLASHED A THIRD time, Brenda, with some relief, thought she knew what it was. At that same moment, Mom rushed into the room crying, "What's going on?" Kelly threw open the window and roughly pulled a camera with a flash attachment away from a guy who was standing among the bushes outside. "Give me that, you pervert!"

It was David Silver, one of the freshman geeks. He looked surprised and a little hurt, which seemed naive to Brenda. If you go sneaking around people's houses, you have to expect people to be upset. When Donna and Andrea saw who it was, they rushed to the window and called him all kinds of names.

Brenda wondered how such an immature guy could be in high school. She called to him, "Get lost, you smut hound, before we call the police."

David Silver escaped across the front lawn and into the night.

Brenda felt exhilarated. David wasn't really dangerous, but the act of chasing him away seemed like the kind of triumphant thing a heroine in a movie would do. She imagined herself to be strong, and full of virtue.

On the floor, Andrea began to put away her Ouija board. "This thing is too powerful," she said, "I don't think we're ready for it."

Amanda gave a haughty laugh.

If David Silver had not broken their spiritual mood, Amanda's laugh had certainly done it. While they were standing around wondering what to do next, Amanda looked at her watch and shrieked.

"What?" Kelly asked, sounding a little strung out.

"It's after midnight," Amanda said sorrowfully.

Brenda was delighted that Amanda could be upset. It not only gave her a modicum of vengeance, it also meant that Amanda was human, and not just a pretentious machine.

Brenda asked, "So what happens? Frat boys turn into pumpkins?"

"No," said Amanda with some disgust, "they turn into drunken slobs." She looked around at them with an evil light in her eyes. "You guys ruined my night," she said, "and now I'm going to ruin yours."

"What are you talking about?" Kelly asked. She, like the rest of them, was apparently made uneasy by Amanda's statement.

Brenda thought of the evil queens in fairy tales who promised to do terrible stuff because they weren't invited to a party, or whatever. She had an illogical urge to burn all the spinning wheels in the kingdom before Amanda could get one of them to prick an innocent finger on the spindle.

Amanda smiled secretively and said in a chummy tone, "Hey, guys, I have a great idea. Let's play Skeletons in the Closet."

"What's that?" Brenda asked cautiously. She had a bad feeling about this, but could see no way to stop the game from happening if the other girls were interested. She didn't want to look like a wuss.

Eagerly, Amanda explained, "Everyone sits in a circle, and the person in the middle has to answer all our questions as honestly as possible."

Brenda glanced at Kelly, who seemed

apprehensive. "What kind of questions?" Brenda asked anxiously.

"Any kind," Amanda said. "Of course, the better the questions, the better the game."

Brenda wondered what Amanda's idea of "better" was. Embarrassing, or just personal?

At first, the other girls weren't sure they wanted to open up that much, but Amanda goaded them into it by suggesting that they had a lot to hide. Or worse yet, nothing to hide.

"This game can get pretty intense," Kelly said.

"Right," said Amanda. "The more intense, the better."

Without knowing why she said it, Brenda said, "Okay. I'm there." Sure, she thought. Why not? The chance of hearing something juicy from someone else and yet protecting herself, though she knew she had nothing to hide, would be an exciting challenge. Dancing on the knife edge appealed to her. This was exactly the sort of thing they were here for.

They sat on the floor in a circle, and Kelly volunteered to go first. From duty, Brenda thought. Noble girl.

Under gentle prodding, Kelly admitted that her middle name was Marlene, and that her favorite color was fuchsia, which Brenda thought was a little bizarre, but was likely, knowing Kelly.

The questions disgusted Amanda. She said,

"Come on, gang. The name of the game is Skeletons in the Closet, remember?"

"We're just warming up," Brenda said.

A moment later Andrea asked, "Kelly, what was your first sexual experience?"

Amanda leaned back in her chair and folded her arms, satisfied.

"Leave it to a reporter," Kelly said.

"Inquiring minds want to know," Andrea said.

Kelly sighed and launched into a long story about her and Steve. They'd been going together for a while, and pretty soon all they could talk about was "doing it." Mostly they talked about where and when. Kelly wanted Steve to rent a suite at the Bel Age Hotel. They would do it in front of a roaring fire. Actually, they ended up doing it in Steve's room while his mom was downstairs being interviewed by "Entertainment Tonight." "They even talked to Steve afterward. You should see the tape! He has this grin the whole time they're talking to him."

That got a huge laugh. Maybe this wouldn't be so bad after all. Brenda had not yet had a sexual experience. What could they possibly ask her about?

In her prodding voice, Amanda said, "Why don't you tell them about your real first time, Kelly?"

Kelly stiffened, but she said, "That was the first time, Amanda."

"What about Ross Webber?"

Of course, everybody wanted to know who Ross Webber was.

And Kelly told them. She began calmly enough, but by the time she finished she had tears in her eyes and Brenda was shocked. The other girls were very quiet, too.

When she was in the ninth grade, long before her nose job, Kelly had had a crush on Ross Webber, this "total godly stud" on the football team. She went to all the games and hung around with the cheerleaders, hoping to get close to him. Then one night, after her school had won a big game, she got her wish. They drove up to Mulholland in a big group. Everybody but her was drunk. Ross wanted to show her "his favorite spot." So she followed him out into the woods, where they had sex. On the ground. Without a blanket.

"After that, he took me home." Kelly sniffed. "And he never spoke to me again." She turned to Amanda and asked, "Is that what you had in mind?"

Amanda only smiled widely and said, "Who's next?"

Brenda thought she was safe. Amanda didn't know anything about *her*. Still, she had no urge to go before her time. Thank goodness Andrea said, "I'll go."

Andrea and Kelly traded places. Andrea

looked composed and ready for anything, as if she were taking some kind of oral test to get into college. She was smart. Brenda didn't have to worry about her.

Amanda hit her with a question she could never have expected. "Why does everybody call you *Ahh*ndrea?"

"Excuse me?"

"Are you British or what? I mean *Ahh*ndrea is so pretentious."

"It's pronounced both ways. I like to be different."

"Good answer," Brenda said.

"Thank you. Am I done?"

"Not yet." Amanda considered for a moment and then asked, "So, have you ever slept with a guy?"

Andrea fidgeted, straightened up, and said, "Not yet."

"If you could sleep with any guy in school, who would he be?"

"Come on, I can't answer that."

Amanda said smugly, "If you can't stand the heat, maybe you'd better go home."

Andrea didn't answer for a moment, and Kelly said, "I bet it's Brandon."

Brenda bet the same thing. It was no secret that Andrea and Brandon were pals, and maybe a little more. Pushing the relationship a step further didn't take much imagination.

"No," said Andrea.

The other girls looked at her incredulously.

"It would have to be Hans Fleishman, this totally gorgeous lifeguard who pulled me out of the water after I got stung by a jellyfish at Zuma Beach last summer."

Having escaped any major damage, Andrea looked ready to flee, but Amanda stopped her by asking, "What is your deepest, darkest secret?"

Andrea and Amanda glared at each other for a long moment. Then Andrea laughed and said, "Okay, you got me. It *is* Brandon. Okay?"

The tension was broken. All the girls but Amanda laughed and claimed they knew it all the time.

"You mean," said Amanda, moving in for the kill, "that it's *not* a secret that you live out of district and lie about your home address?"

Not three people in the school knew this about Andrea, and Brenda was shocked to hear Amanda say it out loud, more or less in public. It had never occurred to her anybody would sink so low.

In a tiny voice Andrea asked, "Who told you that?"

"Kelly," Amanda said.

"Kelly, how could you?" Brenda asked.

"Brenda, how could *you*?" Andrea asked.

As far as Brenda could tell, the only thing

she'd done wrong was presume that Kelly could keep a secret. Which is what she said.

"It's a mistake anyone could make, *Brenda*," Kelly said.

"I don't believe you guys," Andrea cried.

Brenda made them all swear a solemn oath that Andrea's big secret would never leave the room. She didn't know if such an oath would be binding on Amanda, but short of applying a muzzle, it was the best Brenda could do. If word got out, well, they would think of something.

"I want to be next," Donna said.

"Be my guest," Andrea said, and stood up a little unsteadily. Brenda didn't blame her.

As soon as Donna sat down, Amanda began to pick at her. She asked Donna about big secrets, about sexual perversions, about guilty pleasures. Mostly, Donna shrugged and said she didn't know. She did admit that she liked popcorn with her ice cream, but that was hardly in the same league with the stuff Amanda had extracted from Kelly and Andrea. If Donna could be believed—and Brenda had never caught her in a lie, not even when it would have been convenient—she had never so much as pilfered a candy bar. And nobody in her family was even crazy.

Donna sighed and said, "We're all really normal."

Brenda thought that in her own innocent way Donna had done what neither Kelly nor Andrea could do. She had beaten Amanda at her own nasty game.

"I guess you're right, Donna," Amanda said. "Your life is totally boring. Anybody who can't dredge up one secret about themselves is either lying or a major zero."

Donna flinched as if Amanda had struck her.

Brenda said, "That's not true. Donna is a very interesting person."

"Maybe," said Amanda. "What are *you* hiding, Brenda?"

Amanda's question was inevitable. "Nothing," Brenda said, and wondered if it were true.

"Let's find out," Amanda said.

As Brenda took the hot seat, she predicted in her own mind that the next few minutes would be educational for everybody.

13

Bonding, female bonding

BRENDA WAS REALLY GLAD THAT NONE of her friends had Amanda's killer instinct. Or if they did, she was glad they kept it under control. Kelly asked her to tell something outrageous that she had done.

Brenda entertained them with an event of the previous summer back in Minnesota. A mixed party had gone down to a lake. The guys tried to convince the girls to go skinny-dipping, but the girls refused to fall for such a transparent ploy. While the guys were in the water, Brenda and the other girls stole their clothes and their bathing suits. In order to get back to the car the guys had to borrow a blanket from a family having a picnic.

This got a big laugh from everybody except Amanda, who was not impressed. She suggested Brenda tell them a dark secret. Brenda was about to say that she had none, but she didn't want to look like poor, innocent, boring Donna.

Brenda said, "Okay. In the second grade, I used to steal this girl's ice-cream money. And every afternoon I'd watch her cry while I ate an Eskimo Pie I bought with her money."

Donna said, "Brenda Walsh, public enemy number one."

"You should write headlines for the paper," Andrea said.

They all laughed at that, but Amanda still wasn't satisfied. She accused Brenda of pretending she was perfect, better than the rest of them. It wasn't true, of course; she was neither perfect nor pretending to be perfect. Still, Brenda felt that she somehow had to defend her honor. And evidently the only way she could do that was by telling a really horrible story on herself.

"Anything else?" Amanda asked.

"Yes," said Brenda. She told them the story of her greatest regret. Back in Minneapolis, her best friend, Marjorie Miller, was going out with this real cute guy named Doug Fairchild. At a party, Brenda and Doug found themselves alone and they kissed. Brenda liked the kissing, but she knew she shouldn't do anything about it, so she didn't. A few days later, Doug called her and asked for a date.

"I asked him if he was still going out with Marjorie, and he said, 'sort of.'"

So they went out. Brenda lied to Marjorie and said she was staying home that weekend. But Doug took Brenda to a movie at the mall and they were seen.

"Marjorie called me really late. She woke up the whole house. She asked me over and over again how I could do such a thing to her. And the really terrible part is that I know why I did it. I did it to break them up."

It was quiet for a long time after that. Even Amanda seemed to be impressed by Brenda's story. Then Kelly said that she had a confession to make. "After you started going out with Dylan, I tried to get a date with him."

Silence. Universal astonishment. Brenda felt totally betrayed.

"I always liked him, too, Brenda. He flirted with me all last year before you moved from Minnesota."

"Did you ever go out?"

"No."

"Then I guess he wasn't interested." Brenda tried not to sound smug, but she could not help feeling relieved.

"How would you know?" Kelly asked defensively. "Did he ever say anything?"

"I don't know how to break this to you, Kelly," Brenda said, "but when Dylan and I go out together, we definitely don't talk about you."

"I get the message, Brenda. I just thought that after your story, you would understand."

"Understand that you were trying to put the moves on my boyfriend?"

By this time, Brenda and Kelly were shouting in each other's faces.

"I don't believe you guys," Andrea said. "I thought I was going to make some good friends here, but instead I am reminded why I keep to myself. The way things are going, I'm lucky if they don't throw me out of school on Monday." She looked at Amanda. "Right?"

Amanda shrugged and did not seem concerned.

Andrea stood and announced that she was out of there. Kelly said she'd had enough, too, and Donna joined them. They began collecting their stuff. Brenda watched the bonding evaporating before her eyes and she thought rapidly about what she could do to save it. And then the perfect idea came to her. It would rebalance the universe.

"Wait a minute, you guys," she said. "Amanda never sat in the middle of the circle."

"That's right," Donna said. Kelly and Andrea stopped what they were doing.

"Forget it," Amanda said. "Just because you guys fell for my game doesn't mean that *I* have to."

"I wish I hadn't," Kelly said.

"Me too," said Andrea.

Brenda suddenly felt warm toward her sisters, Kelly, Andrea, and Donna. Each thought the others had a perfect life. It turned out that none of them did. Not even Donna's was perfect. Brenda said, "No, I'm glad you did, Kel. I'm glad you shared that really terrible thing with us."

This started a round of apologizing and hugging. Donna was reduced to saying, "I'm sorry for not having more problems. I plan to start having them right away. And when I do, I'll need your shoulders to cry on." She joined the hugging circle. It was only when the front door slammed that they noticed Amanda was gone. The general sentiment was that they were well rid of her.

Then Andrea noticed that Amanda had left behind her purse. Donna picked it up and threatened to throw it out the window. The purse fell open and the contents dumped onto the rug. Among the makeup and the address books and the crumpled tissue were enough pills to start a pharmacy.

Kelly scooped up a few of them. "These are diet pills, amphetamines. Mom used to pop them like candy. Kills your appetite and murders your personality." She shook her head.

"What do you mean?" Brenda asked.

"Take too many of these babies and PMS looks like a vacation."

"Hello?" Amanda stalked back into the house and caught them huddled around her purse. "Give me that," she shrieked. "I can't believe you went through my private things."

Kelly poured the pills back into the purse and handed it to Amanda. "Why do you do this to yourself?" she asked.

"Not all of us were born beautiful, Kelly. Some of us have to work at it, all right?" She pawed through her purse and then snapped it shut.

More gently, Kelly said, "Amanda, you are beautiful."

"Was I beautiful in the eighth grade?"

"You were pretty."

"I was fat, Kelly. And I swore that I would never be that way again. *No matter what*."

"That junk is turning you into a total bitch, Amanda. When is the last time you ate?"

"What do you want me to do? Blimp out? You know guys don't go for fat chicks."

"You don't have to be fat. But maybe you

should just relax and be whatever you are, without all the drugs."

Amanda laughed insincerely. "Well, I guess you guys got me after all. My skeleton's out. I used to be fat and now I'm thin, but I guess I'm a bitch. Good-bye." She shoved her purse under her arm and turned toward the door.

Brenda's feeling of sisterhood overflowed within her. Amanda was obviously a girl in trouble. In her desperate persistence to acquire and keep a slim body, she had alienated all her friends. Maybe Brenda and *her* friends could make a difference. They could actually help a sister to a better life. The bonding would be a success.

Brenda said, "Please don't go, Amanda."

"I thought you wanted me to leave."

"I guess I did. But not now. I want you to stay the night with us." She glanced at Kelly.

Andrea agreed, "Absolutely, Amanda. We all know what it's like to feel unloved and unwanted."

"Are you sure?" she sounded small and insecure.

Kelly said, "Sure we're sure." Donna agreed. Amanda, looking a little unsure of herself, smiled tearfully and agreed to stay.

When they settled on the floor again—Amanda included—Donna searched through the empty plastic bags. "Are there any more of

those chocolate-covered cookies in the fridge?"
she asked

"I think there's another box," Brenda said.

When Donna rose to get a handful, Amanda
asked if Donna would bring a few for her.

This bonding stuff is trickier than it looks,
Brenda thought. But it's worth the trouble.
Now that she had a minute she wondered how
Brandon and Steve were doing. They couldn't
possibly have had as interesting an evening as
she had.

14

A blast in America's heartland

BRANDON DECIDED THERE WAS ALL
kinds of cold. There was the cold he'd felt in
the jail cell, and the cold of people who turned
their backs on you. At the moment, what he
was feeling was just plain temperature cold.
That and bone weariness. And boredom. You
couldn't forget the boredom.

He and Steve had not spoken much
because there wasn't much to say. Brandon sat
down on a bench near a backstop while Steve
paced out near the driveway. They had been
goofing around this abandoned playground for
what, almost an hour. As far as Brandon was

concerned, they'd been there long enough.

He walked down to where Steve was on guard duty and said, "This is hopeless, dude."

"I don't want to hear it, Brandon. If you want to leave, you can. But I *know* they're coming back."

In a pig's eye, Brandon thought. But he wanted to know how far Steve would go kidding himself. "So, like what do you think they're doing out there with your car?" he asked.

Evidently, this was a question Steve had been asking himself because he answered immediately. "Could be a lot of things. Could be they're getting us some beer. Could be Trina left her purse at the club and there's a line outside and they're having trouble getting in."

Brandon didn't say anything. But he decided that Steve had a real talent for writing fiction.

Desperately, Steve said, "You saw how they came on to us, Brandon. You can't fake that stuff."

"Maybe they're actresses."

"Maybe you'd like a fat lip."

"You can be angry at me, Steve, if it'll make you feel better, but you have to know they scammed us. I'm not going to sit here another minute and listen to you make excuses for them." He walked down the driveway to the street.

"Where are you going?"

"To the police. You can come with me if you want."

Behind him, Brandon heard a sound he'd never heard before, and at first he thought he was hallucinating. Steve was crying. Brandon turned around to watch. Until Steve saw some sense, what else could Brandon do?

Steve whined to himself. "I'm such a moron. I can't believe it. What'll I tell my dad?"

"What about the truth?"

Scornfully, Steve said, "Yeah, right. He'd never let me live this down. And what if people at school find out? I will be totally humiliated." He rubbed his eyes and glared at Brandon. "You have to promise you'll never tell anybody."

Well, that was better than Steve denying it had ever happened. Brandon held his left hand up and said, "Scout's honor."

A smile flickered on Steve's face but quickly faded away. He said, "I've never heard anybody say that before."

Brandon threw an arm around Steve's shoulder. "That's your problem, Steve. These things don't happen to good scouts."

As they walked down the driveway Steve asked, "Is it too late to join?"

They walked along the dark sidewalk toward the lights of the main drag. The abandoned elementary school loomed to one side like a bad dream. All Steve talked about was how he would never again trust a stranger just because she looked awesome in cutoff jeans and high heels.

"From now on I'm dating only nuns," Steve vowed.

"Nuns don't date, Steve."

"All right, then, only girls who don't know how to drive."

"You know what W. C. Fields said?"

"'I'll have another drink'?"

"Besides that. He said, 'You can't cheat an honest man.'"

Brandon could see Steve building up another head of anger. Then Steve sighed and shrugged. "More good scout stuff?" he asked.

"Just think of it as advice from a man who knew his way around a con."

Steve thought that one over. Eventually they came to Wilshire Boulevard. Heavy traffic rolled by under lights bright enough to read a newspaper by. They stood on the corner trying to remember the location of the nearest police station. Downtown Beverly Hills was only a few blocks away.

The civic center had recently been remodeled, and now it looked like a movie set for *Ben-Hur* or something. It was all marble arches and columns, all very simple, classic, and imposing. They found an open doorway with a lot of police cars parked in the red zone out in front.

They went inside and walked across the polished marble floor to a blond woman in a uniform sitting behind a reception desk. The woman was not much older than they were and kind of cute in a hard-jawed, militaristic way. Steve just grinned at her and Brandon could see trouble coming. Steve *could not* pass up a pretty face.

Brandon said, "We'd like to report a stolen car."

"Your car?" the woman asked.

"Mine," Steve said.

She directed them to a Sergeant Fuller, who turned out to be a friendly middle-aged guy who gave the impression that he had heard any story they wanted to tell, and then could match them with a better one. Brandon decided he really couldn't know that much about a guy just by looking at his face.

Sergeant Fuller typed notes into a computer while they told their story. When they were done, he said, "Okay. Let me get this straight. You met these two outside Floodlights."

"Right," Steve said.

"What were you doing at Floodlights?" He glanced at Steve's driver's license on the desk before him. "You have to be twenty-one to get in."

"We were just driving by," Brandon said.

"Right," said Steve, "and these girls came right up to the car."

"And they asked you to drive them to the abandoned elementary school."

"Right," said Steve.

"That's trespassing, you know," Sergeant Fuller said evenly.

Steve got an *oops!* expression on his face, and Brandon felt the same way.

Sergeant Fuller went on, "But we'll let that slide." He looked at the computer screen where he'd typed his notes. "Now, I get a little lost between the heavy petting and the actual theft of the vehicle."

"It wasn't heavy petting," Brandon said. More's the pity, he thought.

"And then one of the girls begged you to let her drive your car?"

"Right," said Steve. "It's all Trina talked about from the second she met us."

"So you let her drive your car."

"Right. Then her friend jumped in and they just kept going." He slid one hand against the other with a slap.

"But you told her she could," Sergeant Fuller said.

"Right," said Steve.

Brandon didn't like the sound of this, but Steve seemed oblivious. He had only one thing on his mind, regaining possession of his car.

Sergeant Fuller said, "She had your consent."

"Well, sort of."

Sergeant Fuller pushed the save key on his machine. On the screen the report went away and was replaced by the city emblem. He turned to them. "Sorry fellows, but that's not car stealing. That's car borrowing." He really sounded sorry, but somehow that didn't help.

Steve was so astonished that he was speechless.

"You can't be serious," Brandon said.

Sergeant Fuller said, "If the car is still missing after forty-eight hours, we can report it stolen. Until then, I'm afraid you don't have a case."

Steve said, "In forty-eight hours those two bimbos from the big house could be tossing back margaritas in Mexico."

"You better hope not," Sergeant Fuller said. "Once a stolen vehicle crosses the border, you can generally kiss it good-bye."

"You said it wasn't stolen," Brandon said. Maybe he shouldn't be a lawyer after all.

"Oh, by the time it gets to Mexico, it would be."

Brandon and Steve looked at each other, silently commiserating about the hidden traps in even the best laws. Brandon couldn't let Steve talk. Steve would just explode all over the office and forever screw their chances of getting help from the police. Politeness, however painful it was, was the key.

"So what do you suggest?" Brandon asked.

"I suggest you hope that those two girls do something stupid and that we catch them at it."

"Right," said Steve. He arranged for Sergeant Fuller to call Brandon if the police heard anything. Steve didn't want the police getting his mom by mistake. They shook hands all around and Sergeant Fuller walked them back through the maze of government-green corridors to the lobby.

"What do we do now?" Steve asked.

"You heard what Sergeant Fuller said. We wait for Shelly and Trina to do something stupid."

"They already did something stupid," Steve said, and smashed his fist into his open palm.

Steve's macho bravado was returning. Brandon couldn't decide whether that was good or not. "Can you loan me cab fare?" he asked.

"No problem. Let's get out of here."

They were walking toward the door when Sergeant Fuller ran out to them and said, "I hoped you guys were still here."

"What's the rumpus?" Steve asked.

"We just picked up two girls breaking a hundred in a black late-model Corvette with vanity plates I8A4RE."

"That's my car," Steve cried.

"Very good," said Sergeant Fuller. "We should have them down here in a few minutes."

Steve whooped and the blond woman behind the desk frowned at him. "Yes!" he whispered triumphantly to Brandon.

Brandon and Steve waited in the same room where Sergeant Fuller had taken their statements. Steve nodded in the direction of a guy with long straggly hair wearing a black heavy-metal T-shirt. "See that guy drinking coffee over there?" Steve asked Brandon.

"Yeah?"

"An obvious criminal type. See how close together his eyes are. And one eyebrow that goes all the way across."

The criminal type went out and came back pushing a guy in handcuffs. The guy he was pushing was clean and neat, but had a bruise under his right eye.

Brandon said, "That criminal seems to be an undercover cop."

"Sure," said Steve, making a fast recovery. "An undercover cop has to look like a criminal. Everybody knows that."

After a few minutes Sergeant Fuller came in herding Shelly and Trina before him. Brandon and Steve got to their feet. Steve shouted, "That's them, Sergeant."

"Steve," Trina cried with relief.

"Brandon," Shelly cried.

The girls rushed right over, delighted to see them. Brandon thought this was very strange, considering that in a very few minutes they would be in the slammer. Trina said, "What happened to you guys? We came back and you were gone."

"What are you talking about," Steve asked. "We waited for you almost an hour."

"An hour?" Trina asked. Seemingly confused, she asked Shelly, "Were we gone that long?"

"It didn't seem that long."

Brandon couldn't stand this routine anymore. "Come on," he said. "You guys stole my friend's car."

Shelly said, "What are you talking about, Brandon?"

Hurt and offended, Trina explained that they had just been fooling around. "We went for a ride, but I took a weird turn and we got lost." She turned on the waterworks. While she sniffled and wept she said, "It was so scary. I kept worrying about you guys and wondering if I was ever going to see you again."

Brandon said, "You expect us to buy that load of—"

"Shut up, Brandon," Steve said. There was that bit of a grin on his face that meant he was about to say something he thought was clever. "So, Trina, you think you could make it up to me?"

"Oh, yes," Trina said breathlessly.

Brandon didn't believe any of this. Could Steve really be so naive as to believe these girls were telling the truth about getting lost, about making it up to him, about anything?

Steve asked Sergeant Fuller what condition his car was in.

Sergeant Fuller studied his clipboard for a moment and said, "Clean and in one piece."

"Okay," said Steve. "You can let them go."

"Steve," Brandon said, though he knew it would do no good.

"This one can go," Sergeant Fuller said and nodded at Shelly. "But the one driving the car has a warrant out for her arrest on a prior speeding ticket. Her bail is one hundred and fifty dollars."

"And I'm broke," Trina said sorrowfully.

"Steve," Brandon said again, but it was too late. Steve had already pulled out his wallet. Brandon had no doubt that he was carrying at least $150 in cash.

Outside the police station, Brandon was more than a little cool toward Shelly. He still didn't buy any of this. As far as he was concerned, Shelly and Trina were just a couple of small-time grifters.

But Trina and Steve hugged there on the station steps as if one of them were going off to war. They broke at last and Trina took a sheet

of paper from her purse. Steve turned around
and she used his back for a desk. As she wrote,
she said, "I really appreciate this, Steve. Call
me anytime."

"Sure," said Steve. "How about tomorrow?"

"Great." She folded the paper in four and
handed it to him. She and Shelly waved as
they said good-bye. They trotted down the
steps and soon were out of sight around the
corner of a building. Brandon admitted they
were two fine-looking babes, but they were
carved from solid trouble. He didn't want any
part of them.

"Look at this," Steve said. He was unac-
countably angry again.

Brandon took the paper Trina had given
Steve and read it. He couldn't say he was surprised exactly. It said:

*This certificate good for one deluxe manicure
at Trina's Nails.*

Steve grabbed the paper back and waved it
in the air. "This is not what I meant by making
it up to me." He sank to the steps and shook his
head. "What happened tonight, Brandon? I
thought we had it wired with those girls."

Brandon sat down next to him. "We were
scammed big, bro. But you know what else?"

"What?"

"I had a blast."

It was the truth. He had necked with a very

pretty lady. He had had an adventure that ultimately hurt no one. He had killed an evening by growing up a little. Even when he had been miserable, he'd been having a good time. It was just like TV, only it was better because it was real.

"Sure beats the hell out of a slumber party," Steve said. He handed the certificate to Brandon. "Maybe Brenda can use this."

"Let's go home," Brandon said, and stood up.

In the police lot, Steve went over his car inch by inch looking for dents, scratches, any signs of misuse. He found none. The engine started with a single turn of the key and the gears changed like glass.

"A good thing, too," he said. "Trina wouldn't be hard to find. Her 'nails' are probably in the phone book."

Brandon wondered if a place called Trina's Nails even existed. It occurred to him that Shelly and Trina might not even be their real names. He kept these thoughts to himself.

On the way home, Steve spouted more talk about dates with nuns and being more careful in the future about who he let drive his car. He still stung a little from letting David Silver drive him home from Marianne Moore's house at the beginning of the semester.

"I only did it because I'd had a little too much to drink."

"I remember," Brandon said. Steve didn't really want to hear anything from him. He was having too good a time alternately confessing his mistakes, vowing to do better in the future, and inventing revenge for people he felt had done him dirt. When Steve dropped him off, they shook hands solemnly.

Brandon stood on his front lawn for a moment, listening to Steve's engine disappear in the distance. The air was mild and smelled good. You didn't get this kind of balmy evening in Minnesota in the fall. In the streetlights and porch lights, the white stucco houses around him looked like big blocks of expertly land-scaped sugar. Some people would call this par-adise. No doubt it was a nice place to live, but paradise? Brandon didn't think paradise existed on this planet.

Outside the door, Brandon took off his shoes. He was tiptoeing across the foyer when Brenda called to him from the living room in a loud whisper. He stepped across and saw the room was strewn with sleeping bags, each one with a sleeping girl inside.

"Brandon," Brenda called again.

Brandon stepped over bodies while he thought of all the guys who would die to be in this room right now. It wasn't as exciting as those guys might think. All he saw were lumps in the darkness. He sat down on the couch near Brenda.

She sat up. "Where were you all night?" she asked.

"Out with Steve."

"Doing what?"

"You know, guy stuff. Did you guys bond?"

"I guess."

"Meaning what?"

"Meaning that if you tell me, I'll tell you."

It was the usual stalemate. Brenda would tell him about it eventually, just as he would tell her. Now that the car was back, Brandon didn't think it would matter to Steve if the story got out. And it might not get out, not even if he told Brenda.

"Forget it," Brandon said firmly. "I don't even want to know what girls do when they bond."

"Good. I never would have told you anyway."

Brandon stood up and looked at the stairway to the second floor. Catching a few Zs seemed like a good idea right now. "Good night, Brenda."

"Good night, Brandon," Brenda whispered back.

From somewhere in the darkness came Kelly's voice. "Good night, John-boy."

The silence shattered into laughter that came from all over the room.

Yeah, thought Brandon. Beverly Hills, the Great American Heartland.

Jason Priestley

EVERY SERIOUS TELEVISION ENSEMBLE
drama has to have what program-makers call a *moral
center*. He's the guy who defines the issues for the
audience, makes the choices, learns the lessons.

Sometimes he's the most handsome guy in the
cast, like Harry Hamlin on "L.A. Law." Other times
he's not, like Daniel J. Travanti on "Hill Street Blues."
On "Beverly Hills, 90210," he's blue-eyed Jason
Priestley, and if he's not the handsomest, who is?

Brandon Walsh is often seen looking perplexed.
His parents have given him a code to live by, but living by that code sometimes seems impossible in
Beverly Hills. Brandon continually bends under the
pressures of affluence and idleness, but he hasn't
broken yet . . .

Shannen Doherty

SHANNEN HAS HAD SUCCESS WRITTEN ALL over her from an early age. She was always focused straight ahead, and she has consistently struck her co-workers as determined, knowledgeable, and competent.

Although anyone can see at a glance that she's stunningly beautiful, she's never been one to coast on her looks. Other pretty girls waited for things to come to them; Shannen reached out and grabbed the goodies.

Oddly, she isn't quite convinced that she's beautiful. She's like Brenda, who, when her mother calls her beautiful, answers, "Not California beautiful." Shannen's word for herself is "unusual-looking." True, but the word should be "unusually good"...

Luke Perry

WHY DOES LUKE PERRY ATTRACT THE MOST
fan mail of any "Beverly Hills, 90210" star? His part
isn't the biggest, but Dylan McKay has a wounded-
puppy quality. He's handsome as the devil, but he
doesn't seem to know it. He's cool to be kind. He's
been around and sometimes seems a thousand
years old. Dylan is one of those tormented creatures
who rouse the mothering and loving instincts in
most female viewers, without scaring off the young
men watching.

Luke himself has a past, and he's quite frank in
disclosing his checkered career in school back in
Ohio. Now far beyond that schoolboy rebellion, he's
grown into a level-headed young man with plenty of
reserves to handle all the attention he's getting . . .

Jennie Garth

WHEN KELLY TAYLOR FIRST APPEARED ON screen in "Beverly Hills, 90210," viewers braced themselves for a thoroughly unsympathetic character. She wore the clothes of a villainess, and she had the position and manner of a character who could only mean trouble for naive newcomer Brenda Walsh.

But the producers of the show were more clever than that. When casting the show, they foresaw that even the queen of West Beverly could turn out to have a heart. They chose an actress who could simulate the pettiness of a high school snob while crying out between the lines, "I'm actually nice!"

Ian Ziering

IF YOU'RE LOOKING FOR A LAUGH, STICK with Ian Ziering. His vigor keeps the "Beverly Hills, 90210" cast and crew alert and smiling even when the workday reaches the pumpkin hour. All of his co-workers come out spontaneously with comments like Shannen Doherty's: "Ian is an original. Ian Ziering is the funniest man alive!"

It isn't that Ian talks a lot. That's Jason's job. What Ian does is smile incessantly, as if he's just thought of the biggest joke in the world and he's about to let everybody else in on it. There's isn't an ounce of shyness in Ian. He is up front all the time . . .

Tori
Spelling

TORI SPELLING'S PERSONALITY DOESN'T
leap out at you. A little at a time, it trickles out from
behind her shy exterior. Then before you know it,
you're both smiling and laughing and discussing
something goofy like the latest gruesome horror
movie!

Among the "Beverly Hills, 90210" cast, Tori is
the quiet one. She dresses to not stand out. She
understates herself in her manner and choice of
clothes, confident that you'll see what's inside if you
keep looking . . .

Gabrielle Carteris

GABRIELLE CARTERIS (RHYMES WITH "FAR Paris") is known as Gab on the nickname-happy "Beverly Hills, 90210" set. And Gab does have a tendency to talk. Her physical and verbal energy is irresistible. She's always in the center of the action on the set—chasing Jennie around the scenery, discussing life with Jason, gabbing with Ian.

Her character, Andrea Zuckerman, knows she doesn't fully belong in Beverly Hills or at West Beverly—she uses a fake address. But among the "Beverly Hills, 90210" cast of outsiders, Gabrielle, an outsider from northern California, is in with the rest of them. Andrea can be a moralizing nag, always bringing Brandon up short or forcing him to be more aware of the world outside West Beverly . . .

Brian Austin Green

BRIAN AUSTIN GREEN IS A LOT MORE WISED-
up than dweebish David Silver. He's older—all of
eighteen!—and smoother, but he's still friendly and
eager to please. Don't ask him for an autograph if
you're majorly shy, because he insists on having a
conversation while he writes his best wishes.

Go into the restaurant where he's scheduled a
sit-down with you. Another TV personality might
slam-bang in and announce loudly, "I'm Brian
Green. Show me to my table!" Brian, wearing his T-
shirt proclaiming "World Famous KROQ"—L.A's
top New Wave station—sits on the step outside and
waits . . .

Mel Gilden is the author of over twenty books for children and adults including OUTER SPACE AND ALL THAT JUNK and THE PLANETOID OF AMAZEMENT. He has also written a best-selling novel in the STAR TREK: THE NEXT GENERATION series. He lives in California.

Go back to the beginning...
See the 90 minutes that started it all!

THE BEVERLY HILLS, 90210 HOME VIDEO
available in video stores everywhere January 1992.

Don't Miss An Issue!